CW00841981

SPIRIT IN THE STONES

STONES

THE STORY OF URQUHART CASTLE

A HISTORICAL NOVEL
BY J.A. SNOW

Text Copyright by J.A. Snow 2022. All rights reserved. No part of this publication may be reproduced, distributed, or transmitted in any form without the prior written permission of the author.

In the remote and empty glens herds of wild deer roam and their habit of appearing as if from nowhere is described in a Gaelic phrase. Descending from the mountains and the high passes, the deer are called *Clann a' Cheo,* the Children of the Mist. Travelers in the north of Scotland might think of clans in the same way, their history only occasionally glimpsed in the distance, fleeting, disappearing into the dense forest and the heather-clad uplands. But it is there, and it is a wonderful, magical story.

Alistair Moffat

COVER PHOTOGRAPHY BY JOHN MORGAN

DEDICATION

To Sir Thomas Urquhart of Cromarty, Scotland,

my distant ancestor and kindred spirit,

who also took up his pen to record our family history,

over four hundred years ago.

PRELUDE

The storm had been brewing all afternoon. As the air grew cooler, the skies were rapidly becoming a charred shade of grey, the clouds getting darker and thicker as daylight began to evaporate behind the tree line of the great glen. Then, somewhere between the dusk and the dawn, there was an eerie moment of silence. An instant later a deluge of Biblical proportions swept across Loch Ness, propelled by savage winds blowing up from the Atlantic. Lightning cracked sharply, shattering the dead air. Thunder rolled and rumbled in from the distance like a stampeding herd of highland cattle. Angry waves began churning up the peat-colored water into frothy mounds and came crashing ashore, slamming against the cliffs with Armageddon-like ferocity. Trees from the shoreline all the way to the woods, buffeted by the fierce winds, began to bend and break in surrender. It was a storm as mighty and as terrifying as any of the bloody battles the old fortress had seen in centuries past, pounding against the already cannon-scarred walls like the blows of a hundred axe-wielding warriors or a line of deadly trebuchets. Everything for miles trembled in its wake.

It raged all that night, and, by morning, the grave injuries inflicted on the ancient castle were starkly evident. The boat landing at the foot of the cliffs was completely gone, swept away by the strong currents, and was now buried somewhere deep in the loch. The stone steps that led down to it had been washed away in the mud, leaving nothing but a gaping wound of eroded soil and scattered rocks behind. Above, within the crumbling battlements, fruit trees were uprooted and lying prostrate on the flattened blades of grass. The lowest point of the rolling bailey had become a murky puddle filled with debris and atop the motte everything had been stripped and blown away that was not fastened or weighted down before the storm.

The great tower that had once stood tall and proud on the northern promontory was now nothing but a mutilated finger of ravaged stone, rising pathetically to salute the dawn, its inner stairwell exposed, as if the flesh had been ripped viciously from its lifeless skeleton. Faded, frayed, abandoned draperies fluttered from the open gashes in the stone walls like surrendering flags of truce. Gone were the lovely slate turrets that had for centuries glinted silver in the rising sun; they were now dashed and shattered into tiny pieces on the rocks below. Across the courtyard lay the tattered relics of residents past, strewn about like a child's game pieces, as a horde of human scavengers rushed in to strip it even more. The herd of timid red deer that frequently grazed in the tall grass and warmed themselves in the sunny spots had fled for the hills. The old castle was finally gone.

Or *was* it?

CHAPTER ONE "THE CEARDANNAN"

Annie Urquhart froze in place when she heard the insistent pounding on the door that made the walls around her tremble. All alone in the tiny, two room hovel the family called home, along a row of identical wattle and daub dwellings on Bank Street that led down to Cromarty Firth, she tiptoed across the stone floor and gingerly turned the skeleton key in the lock, trying not to make a sound. She grimaced, knowing she had not been stealthy enough when immediately there was another loud knock on the other side, followed by angry words.

"I know you're in there, Lassie," said the voice. "Tell your Da if I dinnae' get the rent by tonight I will return tomorra' and bring the constable with me!"

Annie held her breath for a few moments until the voice went away and her heart slowed to a quiet flutter before she returned to her broom and pan next to the tiny hearth and resumed her chores, silently cursing her father for drinking away the rent money again. Every month it was the same; the landlord would come calling for his payment that had been squandered away in the town tavern. It was not that George Urquhart was a *lazy* man. He and her older brothers, Angus and Alexander, worked hard, going off early every morning to seek employment of one sort or another. But every afternoon, the boys would return, and their father would stagger in later, drunk, and empty-pocketed, and the cycle would repeat itself. Today, she decided she would confront him before too much whiskey had passed his lips. She would march down to the docks and demand he give her the rent money! She would shame him in front of the other workers if needed. She did not relish the idea of being on the streets with no place to sleep. Annie had seen enough of the world to know things would never change unless she summoned all her courage and made it so!

She rinsed the ash from her hands and emptied the pan into a bucket near the door, returning to the hearth to replace the spent block of peat with another for a supper fire. She sat down for a moment to remove the black from beneath her fingernails with a sharp knife and removed her soot-stained apron. The rest of the housekeeping would have to wait. This was an urgent matter. Knotting her shawl around her shoulders and opening the door slowly to be sure the landlord had gone she ventured out into the street. Hiking up the skirt of the dress that had once belonged to her mother, she hurried along, skipping over the sewage in the crevice that ran through the middle of the street and headed for the docks. Neighbors greeted her and men she knew tipped their bonnets. She tried to smile back at them, but her jaw was set with determination. Some of the women had been friends to her mother; they had helped Annie along with advice on household tasks after her mother had died. Now, they cast sympathetic smiles at her; in their eyes she always saw pity and she did not like it. She was fourteen now and almost a woman. She was determined not to be silent and helpless any longer.

Annie had only a fractured memory of the woman who had given birth to her. Helen Urquhart had died of the pox while Annie was still a wee bairn, so she had been raised in an all-male household from that point on. Accustomed to hard work at an early age and strong for a girl of her stature, she was still a tiny thing, lean but not skinny, with a shock of bright red hair she kept tied up on her head and eyes the color of the Scotch moss that grew on the sea wall. Physically, she was exactly the opposite of her brothers who looked like identical twins although they were a year apart in age, who were both dark-haired and swarthy. Her father liked to tell folks the boys were conceived at the same time but Angus, who was the shy one of the two, chose to remain in the womb for nine more months before he made his appearance. At the time, Annie did not know much about such matters; now that she was older and knew better, she wrote it off to *whiskey* talking.

She looked up and could tell the fishing fleet was in from the line of furled masts she could see in the foggy distance. Repairs to the sea wall after a storm had been keeping her father and brothers busy for the past several weeks. Masonry was his usual trade, but George Urquhart was not too proud to take any manner of work. Although he preferred building stone walls and houses, he sometimes, if there was nothing else, took odd jobs around town. The recent storm had been a blessing. The harbormaster was a *paying* customer with coin in his pocket. While Cromarty still had unrepaired damages from the never-ending scrimmages with the English and the frequent Jacobite uprisings, not to mention the clashes between the Clans, most of the townsfolk opted to make repairs themselves, a little at a time, as time and money permitted. Most Cromartiens were too poor to pay a mason. The scars of war were everywhere, and some would remain part of the permanent landscape.

Situated on the northern tip of the Black Isle, the name Cromarty meant *crooked bay*, or so she had been told. When Annie looked out over the water now, her eyes told her it was not the *bay* that was crooked at all. The water was only yielding to the land, the true sculptor of the shoreline, filling in the inlets and coves beneath the high rocks called the *Sutors* that stood like the boots of a giant sentry, guarding the entrance to the firth. Her ancestors, many years before, had

9

been the hereditary sheriffs of the royal burgh, a highly respected Scottish clan, and had commanded land and castles from Caithness to Inverness and even parts of Aberdeen too. At least, that was the information she had gleaned from her father's stories. But that was many years before the financial woes of the Clan leader had thrown them into penury and disgrace and the extended family had scattered to the four winds. There were only a handful of Urquharts left in Scotland now, the last of a dying breed.

As she neared the water, she passed a dozen fishwives with hooks in hand, sliding the morning catch across the bloody tables, gutting them with knives that had been honed down to thin daggers, pitching the heads and tails onto the dock where the gulls dove and squawked over the stinking mess. Annie tiptoed through a group of men sitting on the landing mending their nets and tried to ignore their stares. Days were always busy on the docks. The tiny harbor was the heart of Cromarty, beating with the daily activities of its inhabitants. Indeed, it pumped the lifeblood of every family who lived there in and out and kept them alive. It was surrounded by a rock wall that curled around it like a giant scythe and kept the high surf away from the small boats and fishing skiffs moored there.

She found her brothers and her father already covered in mortar and wet to the knees, jockeying the heavy stones into position to replace the broken ones, while the waves lapped beneath them on their makeshift scaffold. Sweat was glistening on their faces and soaking through their shirts. George Urquhart looked up and cocked an eyebrow in disapproval when he saw his daughter.

"What are you doing here, Annie Urquhart?" he said. "Have you not enough chores at home to keep you busy?"

"Aye, I have chores, Da," she replied, placing her hands on her hips defiantly and taking a deep breath to summon her courage. "But I need money to pay the rent. The landlord came a'callin' this mornin' and he says if'n he doesna' have it by today he'll be throwin' us out on the street."

Her father looked down and brushed off his hands, embarrassed to be chastised by his daughter in front of the other men on the docks. "That is my business. Be off with you now. We will speak of it when I get home."

"No," said Annie stubbornly. "We'll speak of it *now*, before you drink your pay away at the tavern! I will not be sleeping in doorways and begging for food at the church! I'm going to stay right here until you give me the rent money!"

An older man with the look of authority walked up behind her father. She recognized Mister Ross, the harbormaster. He was a large, well-built man, stern-looking, and he intimidated Annie with his very presence. "Is there trouble here, Urquhart?"

"Just my disrespectful daughter, Sir. No trouble. She'll be going home now, or she'll be feeling the back of my hand!" George Urquhart shot his daughter another angry look.

The man looked Annie directly in the eye with an expression of disapproval. "Off with you now, Lass. Your Da has work to finish."

Annie's mind raced. She did not want to get her father fired but she knew if she went home, he would surely go to the tavern at quitting time and probably give her a tongue lashing when he got home just for good measure. She took two steps backward and looked to her brother with pleading eyes. "Alex, please *talk* to him," she begged.

Her older brother nodded and approached her, jumping up onto the sea wall and taking her by the shoulders. "I will, Annie. Dinnae' concern yourself. You go on home and tend to your chores like a good girl." He gave her a gentle push to send her on her way.

"But Alex……"

He nudged her again. Defeated, and doubtful that her brother could change their father's behavior no matter how hard he tried, she backed away. Tears began to well in her green eyes and she turned her head so that her father could not see. She was angry and crying only showed her weakness. She walked slowly, back toward the street, avoiding the sympathetic stares of the people she passed. When she was far enough away, she stopped, closing her eyes for a moment, and pulled her hair up on the top of her head to let the cool breeze off the water embrace the back of her neck. The air was already warm with the sun that had burned off the morning mist. Today would be a hot one and the little house would be stifling by noon. Best to get her chores done early and she had already wasted enough time on this fool's errand.

When she opened her eyes again, she looked beyond the rooftops at the giant fortress on the hill looming over a hundred feet above the town; old Cromarty Castle stared down at her like a disapproving mistress, the six-story tower of antiquity surrounded by trees and moss-covered grey walls that was always a constant source of fascination to her. It was hard for her to believe that her family had once been important enough to have lived within those walls, that her ancestors had looked out from those battlements over the home where they now lived in squalor, in the runoff from the castle sewer, quibbling over rent money they did not have. She had ventured up the hill many times in her youth, through the deep ravine that surrounded it, climbing up to sit with her back against the cold stone wall where she could see for miles and daydream for hours, watching the bottlenose dolphins splashing in the firth and the gulls gliding on the wind. She could not explain what drew her there. Many residents had passed through the castle gates in the centuries since it had been built. Many standards had flown on the mast that waved above the giant portcullis. Someone else controlled it now, most likely creditors or the tax collectors. Above the battlements now flew an English flag, and it was occupied by red coated soldiers who frequently marched through town and berthed their ships in the harbor. The great gates were kept locked to everyone except those garrisoned there. In all her fourteen years, Annie had never seen behind the walls although her imagination told her it was a magical place, a place that had been taken from her family long ago, and it made her sad. She sighed and put it out of her mind as she made her way home.

Once inside, housekeeping chores and supper preparation kept her busy until it was time for her brothers to return from the docks. After she had darned Alex's socks and sewn the loose buttons back on Angus' shirt, she made up the four tiny beds, shook the dust out of the rugs and put a kettle on to boil for supper. The sun was now glaring through the tiny window that faced the street, illuminating the folds of blackened thatch that hung between the eaves above the hearth. Annie watered the tiny potted rosebush she had started from a wild cutting and turned its withered leaves toward the waning sunlight. She felt a bit like the little plant, couped up within four dreary walls, longing for the aroma of green grass and trees outdoors. She could smell the unpleasant stench from the sewer creeping through the open door, and she wrinkled her nose. There would be no time for walks up castle hill today. She had already wasted enough time.

When Alex and Angus finally came through the door later that afternoon they were as weary as usual and headed straight for the cask of ale in the corner to quench their thirsts after a long day of work.

"Where is Da?" she asked, already knowing what the answer would be.

The boys both sat down at the rickety table, and she took them bowls of the fish stew she had prepared. She never thought of her brothers as particularly handsome. While they were both rugged and strong, they were not like the English soldiers who pranced around town in their crisp uniforms. Her brothers were of good Scottish stock, with the rawboned ruggedness of Highlanders, even if their clan *had* been too weak to survive. Alex was her hero; she always felt safe when he was around. He had defended her many times, keeping her out of harm's way when her father was on a drunken binge, cursing and swinging at everything in sight. He could always make her laugh even when she felt sad. She did not have the same feelings for her other brother, Angus, who was sullen and brooding most of the time and rarely spoke to her unless it was necessary.

After two or three bites Alex finally answered. "I spoke to him, Annie. We are leaving Cromarty," he said. "Even with today's pay we still won't have enough for the rent. We are to pack up all our belongings and leave tonight."

His words stunned Annie. "Leaving? Going where? We have no place to go! Will Da have us wandering in the streets like the gypsies?"

Her brother looked at her with apologetic eyes and reached out to take her hand. "Dinnae' worry, Lass. We will find work somewhere. We won't let you starve, little sister."

"I'm not a'worryin' aboot starvin'," she replied. "But where are we going to *sleep*? Outside the taverns along the way while Da drinks away his pay? It will get mighty cold come winter!"

Alex shook his head and shrugged his shoulders. "I did my best. He *is* still the head of this family."

"Well, maybe he shouldna' be then! When will one of you stand up to him?"

Again, Alex patted her hand. "Angus and I will protect you. There was talk on the docks that the Ceardannan are in town. Da says we can join up with them and find work up the road."

Annie went livid. She burst into tears and ran out of the house, flinging herself down on the porch step. This was fine then! The family had surely reached the bottom of the well if her brothers spoke of joining up with the highland gypsies! She had heard what a lot of thieves and pickpockets they were, going from town to town, selling their shoddy wares and stealing anything that was not bolted down. She thought of her mother and wondered what she would have done if she were still alive. Surely her father would not have condemned his wife to such a life! Alex followed a few paces behind her and sat beside her on the stoop.

"Gettin' yerself so upset will not change things, Annie. We just dinnae' have enough money to stay here. But we'll find work. You needn't worry yerself."

"We never have enough money because Da spends it all on whiskey! Dinnae' you see, Alex? It is all his fault! What would our mum say? She wouldna' put up with it. She wouldna', I tell ya!"

15

Alex shook his head. He remembered life when their mother had still been alive, before their father had begun to drink so heavily. He was not at all sure things would be any different if their mother were still with them. Annie was too young to recall the drunken beatings their mother had endured before she was born.

"Think of it as an *adventure*." Angus spoke suddenly from the doorway, grinning.

Annie reeled on him. "*Adventure*? Are you *mad*? Can you *hear* yourself? You want to live with thieves and unwashed heathens? You want to sleep in the dirt and mud when the rains come? Have you no pride in our family name? Our ancestors were once sheriffs in this town! They once lived in that castle on the hill. Now, look at us!" She sniveled and pointed up the street where dim lanterns now flickered from within the deep-set stone windows.

Alex took a deep breath. His shoulders slumped. He felt the shame too; even though he would not show it to his father, it was there, just under the surface. His face was rigid and his voice did not crack from emotion. "We didna' have a choice, Annie. We must get by with our lot the best we can. Those ancestors you speak of didna' leave us anything. That is why the English flag flies up there instead of the Scottish one! Maybe when Bonnie Prince Charlie returns, he will drive the English out of Scotland once and for all."

Annie wiped her nose for the last time. "The English army is not our problem, Alex. *Da* is."

While she cleaned up the supper dishes Alex and Angus packed up the household belongings and were soon ready to go. Bedding was rolled up to be strapped to their backs. Tools of their masonry trade were tucked into packs to be slung over their shoulders. Annie gathered what was left of the food; the last of the bannocks, oats, and dried meats, everything that would not perish in the summer heat. She packed it all into a small burlap bag along with her clothes and her most precious possession: the remnant of a small purple plaid tartan her mother had made for her as a bairn. At night she slept with it between her head and her pillow. She refused to wash it, so it still had the faint smell of her mother nestled in its fibers after all these years, or so Annie imagined. She didn't really remember *what* her mother smelled like. Whatever it was, it was comforting to her. Now it was faded and beginning to unravel, nothing left but a rag.

By the time George Urquhart finally walked through the door his three children were waiting, packed and ready to go; on their anxious faces were the questions he refused to answer as he gulped his lukewarm supper without complaint. Annie had given up the fight. She cleaned up after him and put the bowl in the bag with the other dishes in silence. He had determined their destiny and neither she nor her brothers had a say in it. She tried to avoid her father's eyes. For most of her life she had been invisible to him and yet once or twice she had caught him staring at her, *through* her, as if seeing a ghost.

"Have ye settled yerself down now, Annie? Or must I give ye a lesson in manners? 'Tis a good thing our job on the docks was nigh on finished or Mister Ross would have fired me for sure!"

Alex interrupted, fearful his little sister would start another argument. "Are you sure joining the Ceardannan is the right answer, Da? Are we to put away our tools and become thieves and pickpockets now?"

George glared at his son. "They aren't *all* criminals," he said. "Some of 'em are just hard-working men like us looking for work. There is employment out there when you want it."

17

"Aye," replied Alex. "But is it the proper place to take little Annie? Would Mum have approved?"

George fell silent. He knew Alex had a point, but he had made his decision. As the patriarch of the family, he would not be questioned. There was little conversation as they started out. Her father seemed more sober than usual which surprised Annie. Obediently, she filed out of the house with her brothers but stubbornly lagged behind following them up the street, toward the edge of town. The summer night was balmy, and the moon was big behind them, hovering above the peaks of the Sutors over their shoulders. They followed the southern road, past the little overgrown cemetery where the gravestones glowed eerily in the twilight, past the sleeping bishop's house, towards the thick woods beyond. As it got darker beneath the trees Annie felt a tingle in her spine with every rustle of the leaves. Had it not been for the bits of gravel embedded in the road that sparkled in the moonlight it would have been pitch black. She stumbled as she quickened her pace to catch up.

"Mister Ross said they have a camp just over the hill," Alex said as she fell into step beside him. "We should be able to see their campfires. Surely, they can use three good masons. Dinnae' you worry. We'll make out fine."

Annie was silent, still brooding over what she believed to be a foolish decision on the part of her father. How much lower could they sink? From a once noble family to a pack of roaming gypsies! She hoisted her bundle higher on her shoulders and trudged forward up the dark road until the predicted campfires appeared in the distance.

There they were, gathered around a raging pile of rowan wood, encircled by a ring of dilapidated wagons, strange faces with dark eyes shining in the firelight, voices in song, music squealing from a fiddle and a tired bagpipe. The music and singing stopped when her father walked right up as if he owned the place.

"Name's George. These are my sons, Alex and Angus. We heard you could use some masons in your crew."

One man sitting at the fire, tall and broad-shouldered, wearing a faded, grey kilt that showed no clan affiliation stoked the fire without looking up. "Where you from?"

"Cromarty," replied George, "the house of Urq...."

"We dinnae' use *clan* names here," the man interrupted. "We aren't lookin' fer trouble. You ain't Jacobites, are ya?"

George Urquhart cleared his throat nervously. He knew there were many Scots who considered those who followed the Catholic Prince Charles to be rebels, but he had not expected bigotry from a bunch of gypsies.

"No, Sir. Just unemployed masons lookin' fer honest work."

"We might could use a mason or two. There's talk of work down south of here and rich lairds with money to spend." He paused to poke again at the fire at his feet. "If'n you join us there will be rules to abide by."

George's eyebrows raised slightly. "Rules, you say?"

"Aye," said the man. "We dinnae' take on freeloaders. Everyone works for their keep. Even the wee lass there." He pointed at Annie with the charred stick in his hand.

"We are not afraid of hard work," replied George. "We are not beggars. I just finished work on the Cromarty docks and there's not much other work to be had. Time to move on."

Annie frowned at him for telling such a tall tale. *There was plenty of work in Cromarty*, she thought dismally, *and unfortunately plenty of whiskey too.*

Satisfied, the man stood up and faced them. "Geoffrey." He extended his hand.

George took his hand and pumped it enthusiastically. He and the boys took their places by the fire and Annie wandered off and made herself comfortable against the trunk of a nearby tree. She refused to be part of this bunch of thieves and pickpockets and chose to remain aloof. Disgusted, she watched from a distance as her father began his storytelling and soon had his new comrades laughing at his jokes. As the fire dwindled, and the liquor jug was passed around, the men began to wander off to their beds. Finally she pulled out her mother's tartan, laying it carefully across her bag, and rested her head upon it, closing her eyes and wishing for sleep to escape the nightmare around her.

Morning was busy and it was obvious the Ceardannan did not tarry long in one place. There was no morning fire, no liquor, no laughter, only the labor of packing up and moving on. Breakfast would be consumed on the road. In the daylight Annie could now clearly see the people that belonged to the eyes around the fire. Men and women scurried around her, as the campsite was swept clean of bedding and eating utensils and the wagons were loaded up. Her father and Angus, who had fallen asleep near the fire, were shaking the leaves and dirt from their bed sacks. Alex apparently had slept on the grass at her feet and was just waking up. He caught her glance and shot her an apologetic smile.

"Were you able to sleep with all the carrying on last night?" he asked as he dug in the bag for a cold bannock.

"I slept all right. But I still think this is madness, Alex. Cannae' you *reason* with him? There is still time to go back to Cromarty. We've managed to survive there for a long time now."

"I kept an eye on you last night," he said, ignoring her question. "I'll be sure no one bothers you, if that is what you fear."

Annie laughed out loud, although she saw no humor in it. "Aye, when you didna' have your eye on that whiskey jug. I saw ya! Sucking it down like a pig on the teat. You'd better be careful, or you'll end up a drunk just like Da."

Alex grinned sheepishly. "I have a wee bit of a headache this mornin'.'"

"And you deserve it, going along with this crazy idea. Only the good Lord knows where we'll end up."

She took a bannock for herself and sniffed it before she took a bite. Cold and growing stale in the misty morning air, it was not as pleasant as one fresh and warm from the hearth and it had lost its pungent muskiness from the peat fire. The sights and smells of home were just the beginning of the things Annie would have to forget in this strange new world in which she found herself. She suddenly remembered the little rose bush back home in the window which she had completely forgotten in the rush to move. It would surely die now unless the new tenant was a woman who appreciated such things. Everything was dead about Cromarty now. The docks, the apartment, the little plant in the window, the castle on the hill. Disgusted, she looked across the clearing at her father who was conversing with the man called Geoffrey.

The group began slowly making their way up the road, away from town, away from the only home Annie had ever known.

Wagons stretched out as far as she could see, dilapidated old vehicles with faded bedsheets for covers and crooked, rickety wheels bouncing over the rutted road. Most of the gypsies were on foot shuffling along between the wagons. One wagon passed her driven by a very old man who wore a funny, straw hat that was tall with a wide brim and pointed at the top. He had a long white beard and had a thin, long-stemmed cob pipe dangling from his mouth which gave him the look of a wizard, at least what a wizard *should* look like in Annie's girlish imagination. He seemed to her to be the most interesting person in the group. His trade was apparent from the rows of wicker baskets and straw brooms strung across his wagon. The rest of the people seemed to be raggedy wanderers, clad in dusty clothes and carrying soiled bundles and a variety of tools over their shoulders. There was a rumble of conversation among them that was garbled, and she could not understand some of it until she realized many of the gypsies were speaking Gaelic, the ancient language of the Highlands, a language that was familiar to her ears but foreign to her tongue. She wondered how far away they had wandered from *their* homes to be a part of this motley crew. Looking back down the road in the light of morning toward Cromarty she wondered about the new world she was going to see. Would it be a friendly or hostile place? While a tiny part of her was curious about what lay ahead, she still harbored her resentment at being uprooted so suddenly, at being forced into a bunch of strangers.

"Come now, Annie," Alex said quietly, approaching her from behind and falling in step beside her. "Maybe Angus was right, and it *will* be an adventure." Her sour expression left no doubt what she thought regarding *that* idea.

They walked for a half a day it seemed without seeing anyone else travelling the road, only a flock of sheep grazing in the tall grass and a pair of Highland ponies that lifted their heads curiously when they passed by. The wizard's horse whinnied at them, and they whinnied back. At one point the road rose to an elevation from which they could see all the way back to Cromarty. Annie did not want to look back, but the temptation was too great. At a distance, the houses looked like tiny white specks against the blue of the firth, the masts of the ships in the harbor sticking out like pins in a cushion. Only the old castle on the hill was distinguishable in the distance, still watching over the town, strong, unmoving, steadfast. Nothing, even the view from afar, could diminish its stately appearance. She felt tears in her eyes and turned to face the road ahead.

Soon they changed direction, where the road dropped down and ran beside a long body of water. They passed through several small fishing villages. George joined a few of the men who stopped to inquire about employment. Not only was there no work to be found, a few of the townsfolk also came out of their houses and shouted at them as they passed. "Get on with ya' gypsy rabble!" Annie heard one of them say. "Keep movin'! Nothing to steal here!" yelled another. Annie glanced at Alex and saw the look of embarrassment in his dark eyes.

"Dinnae' worry yerself, Annie. Just ignore it. If not here, we'll find work up the road."

They kept walking the remainder of the day, until they reached a quiet stretch of sandy beach near a small boat landing and decided to camp for the night. The sun was ebbing behind the mountains and a mist was slowly creeping in over the water. Annie was glad they decided to stop for a rest. She could feel blisters oozing between her toes. Her face was parched from the sun and the mist felt cool on her skin. As the group fanned out to set up camp, the men unharnessed the horses and pitched tents while the women drug out pots and pans and cleared a spot to build a fire and prepare food. Alex went in search of their father who was far ahead with his new friends. Annie was tempted to find a spot on the sand and take a nap for she had not slept as well the night before as she had told her brother. In truth, her sleep had been fitful; she had spent hours tossing and turning at the strange human voices across the campsite and the wild animal sounds coming from the woods.

"You too, Lassie!" A stout, middle-aged woman was standing above her, hands on her hips, eyes blazing. "Your Da was told we *all* work in the Ceardannan! Up with you now and gather wood for the fire!"

Startled, Annie stood up and immediately reached down to retrieve her knapsack.

"No need to carry that with ya," said the woman. "We dinnae' steal from our own."

Annie dropped the bag reluctantly, more worried about leaving her mother's tartan behind than of having their food stolen, and started out, searching the grass and scrub bushes for wood. All of her life she had built their fires from peat. She had no knowledge of wood fires, but common sense told her they would need kindling, so she began gathering twigs and sticks, stuffing them into her rolled up apron. Others were wandering too, stooping, and filling their aprons. One woman who was heavy with child was using her skirt, filling it with wood, revealing a pair of red knobby knees, although bending and stooping seemed to be difficult for her.

"Can I help you carry your wood, Mum?"

The woman shot her a grateful smile. "Thank ye," she mumbled.

She had a kind face, but Annie was not prepared to make friends with the gypsies. She was only being polite.

"What's your name?" the woman asked.

"Annie…." She stopped and remembered: *No clan names*. In the Ceardannan they were to remain anonymous as to their political alliances to keep the peace.

"I'm Deidre. I believe you met my husband, Geoffrey."

"Travelling must be hard on you, carrying a bairn and all," said Annie.

"Oh, it's not so bad. My auld man has made me a comfortable bed in the wagon. I just cannae' seem to bend over anymore." She laughed.

Annie approached her and transferred the woman's wood into her own apron. "Here, at least let me lighten your load for ya."

 Although she would never admit it, some of the gypsies were turning out to be more normal than she had anticipated. Deidre gave her a grateful smile. "You came with those boys from Cromarty, didnae' ye?"

"Aye."

"Where's your Mum?"

Annie shrugged. "She died when I was little. It's just me and Da and my brothers now."

 "Oh, I'm so sorry."

"We manage alright." Annie nodded and moved on, stifling the conversation, collecting more wood until her apron could hold no more. After she returned to the campsite and deposited her load with the others, she went back out to find more.

25

Wandering toward the shore, she saw the wizard had removed his strange hat and was using it to carry water to his horse. *Silly auld man*, thought Annie, wondering why he did not unhitch the horse and lead it down to the water like all the others. It would make ever so much more sense than carrying the straw hat back and forth while it leaked like a sieve. The poor horse drooped under the weight of the wooden yoke of the wagon accepting each hatful with weary indifference. Annie doubted the poor animal would last the journey. She approached and reached out to rub his furry ears.

"Excuse me, Sir," she said politely when the old man came close. "Would you like help unhitching your horse? Surely it would be easier to let him drink from the water's edge than to cart it back and forth like that."

The old man looked up and stared at her, startled, before he went about his business and held his leaking hat up to the horse's nose. "I can manage just fine, Lassie. I dinnae' liken to have my horse eaten by the sea creatures."

Annie's imagination was piqued. "Sea creatures? What sea creature is so large that it could possibly eat a horse?"

The horse drained the hat and the wizard returned to the water's edge to fill it again while Annie followed. "Why the *kelpie!* Dinnae' you know anything aboot *anything*?"

Annie shook her head.

"The kelpies are three times the size of an earthly horse. They eat men and horses alike if they choose!"

Annie smiled. *Faerie tales*, she thought in amusement. "I should like to see one of your sea-creatures, Sir."

The old man stared at her with an incredulous frown. "No, you wouldna'," he mumbled, closing his eyes and whispering something into the air that sounded a bit like a prayer.

She left him then and continued gathering wood until her apron was full again, adding it to the pile near the center of the camp. No one else spoke to her. Everyone was busy with their own personal chores. Having done what was requested, she wandered further up the shore and sank down on the bank. Looking out over the cool blue of the loch, she thought about the old man's sea creatures. She could see a town on the opposite side, ahead, just up the beach from the camp, where there was a platform and a small landing from which ferry boats were coming and going. On the other side, behind the docks and ships moored there, she could see it was no fishing village; grand houses dotted the horizon, much larger than any in Cromarty, and many people scurried in the street. Above the town was another large castle reminiscent of *their* castle in Cromarty except that the walls on this one stood much higher, with one great tower peppered with dozens of tall, narrow windows. It was built of stone that was a reddish color almost the shade of rusty iron and the setting sun burned upon it like flames. It was surrounded by rugged cliffs of speckled granite. The great gate was standing wide open, and the portcullis had been raised. Annie could only hope they would stay here long enough to explore. It looked like an interesting town, especially the castle. She hoped they would find work there and stay in one place for a while. At that point she saw her father and her brothers on the landing with the other men of the Ceardannan preparing to board a boat to cross over. She jumped up and ran to join them.

"Cannae' I come along too, Da?" she called to them.

George Urquhart turned around and shook his head. "A big city is no place for a lass. We are goin' to look fer work. You stay behind with the women and behave yerself until we return."

Alex reached out and put his hand on his father's shoulder. "Da, we cannae leave Annie to spend the night alone in camp!"

George Urquhart grunted.

"I will stay with her," Alex said firmly.

"No." Geoffrey interjected. "We need all our able-bodied men. The more men we have the more money we can make. Tell the lass to go see my wife. She'll find a place for her to sleep tonight."

Annie and Alex exchanged a worried look.

"I'll be all right, Alex," she said.

Annie did as she was told and returned to the camp where she found the woman named Deidre stirring a cauldron over the fire. She sat down on a rock and stared into the flames.

Deidre remembered Annie's kindness that afternoon and smiled at her.

"Your Da and your brothers off to Inverness?"

Annie nodded.

"Well, there is room for you in our wagon tonight. Come and eat, Child. The men will be back soon enough."

CHAPTER TWO "OLD KING BREDAI"

Twelve centuries before Annie Urquhart sat on the shore, gazing across the water at the town of Inverness, others were also setting eyes upon it for the first time. There was no impressive stone castle back then, only a wooden fortress of sharpened timbers situated on the same rocky hilltop. It was encircled at the bottom of the hill by dozens of squat, round houses and crude shops with black peat roofs and dry-rock walls where blacksmiths and metalworkers pounded with their hammers, women carted bushels of laundry on their hips back and forth to the water's edge, and farmers' wives laid out vegetables for sale. While not so grand and large as it would be in Annie's time, it was already an important place, alive with the business of the Pictish clan of Fortriu and their king, *Bredai*. Bredai, the son of the great Maelchon, had settled there at the mouth of the River Ness where it sucked water from the great loch. His people had followed and gathered around him. There were other Pictish kings, but none so revered as Bredai. Today, to the king's surprise, he was being visited by an old acquaintance from the island of Ireland.

The vessel that appeared in the harbor that day was a strange one, unlike any the Picts had seen before: a wicker currach covered in leather for watertightness with twelve brown-hooded monks pulling strenuously on the oars. The man at the bow was a striking figure, obviously great in height and powerfully built which was evident even beneath his robe. He had a loud, deafening voice that projected across the water. "Pull! Pull!" he cried out with every stroke. They were crossing the mouth of the river and the swift current was so strong it was trying to suck them into its powerful jaws. "Pull!" the head monk called again until they maneuvered and backstroked on their paddles across the rapids and came close enough to the dock to allow a young boy to throw them a rope and pull them in.

"Thank you, young man," said the big monk as he hoisted himself up with the help of a long, hooked walking stick, speaking slowly in Pictish. "We are here to visit the good king Bredai. Will you allow us to tie up our boat here for a bit?"

The young dockhand shrugged, holding the boat steady so that they could disembark. "No matter to me," he said, staring at the holy men as they stepped onto the platform one by one. "That is a strange boat for sure! Where is it you come from?"

The tall one stepped forward and offered his hand. "I am Columba," he said, slipping fluidly from the Gaelic tongue of Ireland to the Celtic dialect of the highlands again. "*Columbkille* in your language, Son. These are my brothers in the faith. We are from Ireland. We will not be here exceptionally long. Just time enough to extend greetings to my auld friend and be on our way."

Columba was the only one among the monks who was acquainted with the town of Inverness. He turned to the others whose eyes had grown large and apprehensive at the sight of such a large group of Picts. "Do not worry about our safety, Brothers. They are friendly pagans here."

The boy tied up the currach and the one who called himself Columba led the monks away from the water and up the street toward the fortress at the top of the hill. They marched through the village in a silent brown line, in perfect cadence, right steps in sync with each other followed by left steps, all except for Columba with their heads down, eyes on their feet. The boy on the docks watched them until they disappeared like a brown worm into the mound of people in the street. It was always busy this time of day, but he could see the crowd part in the middle, allowing the strange visitors to pass through. The pagan eyes were agog; it was not often that Christian missionaries visited Inverness. The eyes of the monks did not wander, however, at the people with outlandish painted flesh on their bodies, at the pagan amulets they wore around their necks, at the knives and spears lashed to their hips.

The king had been forewarned they were coming by a young boy who had sprinted up the hill with the news only minutes before and he was ready to greet them as soon as they reached the top of the hill. "Open the gates!" he called to his men. "It is my dear friend all the way from Ireland!"

The gate creaked opened and Bredai emerged. Columba gazed upon him for a moment and waved. The king had aged considerably in the years since their last meeting. His hair was now white and very long and his mustache came together beneath his lower lip to form a braid. His face seemed paler and more fissured than Columba remembered, and his chest was naked showing a crop of greying fuzz that covered the colorful pictures painted on his bare skin. Around his waist and throat were heavy iron chains, for in those days iron was more valuable than gold or silver, and on his hip he wore a short spear even though he was surrounded with armed men.

"Columbkille!" he called out happily. "It has been a very long time since I saw you last! Welcome back to my home."

Columba stepped forward and embraced the king warmly. "It has been too long my painted friend. How are your pagan gods treating you?"

Bredai laughed heartily. "They have been good to me. And what of *your* god? Has he blessed you and kept you healthy since we last met?"

Columba grasped the wooden cross that hung around his neck and kissed it in response. It was on his heart to one day baptize the king, but he always avoided preaching to him hoping for a spontaneous conversion. Their discussions of religion were always a playful exchange of different viewpoints. With every visit, both the king and the missionary learned a little more of each other's language.

Arm in arm they climbed the hill and entered through the gate, approaching the king's home followed by the other monks. A long table was being set, and food was frantically being laid out by servants in great haste. The king motioned for them all to sit and eat. He filled his own goblet with wine and held it up in a toast to his visitors. The monks began to pray silently while Bredai and Columba clicked their goblets together.

"Tell me, what news of Dal Riata?"

"We visited there a fortnight ago. Conall Mac Comgaill has been very generous. He has given us a small island on which to build an abbey there. It will act as a home base for our missionary work."

"Hmmmmm," murmured Bredai. "But what of the *wars?* Are the Gaels coming north? My gods are telling me to prepare for an attack."

Columba shook his head. "No, I did not see any military preparations during my visit. In fact, it was very subdued. There has been much sickness and they are burying many poor souls."

The king sighed deeply and drank from his goblet deeper still. "Aye, we have had some of that too. Some days it seems like death approaches me from all sides. If it is not on the tip of an enemy's spear it is from sweats and fevers." He leaned in and whispered in the monk's ear. "How is it you manage to keep so healthy and happy in these dark days?"

It was a golden opportunity for Columba. His mind searched for just the right words. "I have my God, and he is always standing beside me. I am forgiven of all my sins and when I die, I am promised a home with him. There is nothing to fear, my friend, when you believe."

Bredai smiled. "I wish I could accept that, but all the signs tell me of war and death."

"You must stop looking for signs and find faith in the one true God."

The king filled his mouth with food and wine and changed the subject. "Have you heard the stories of our water monster? It is quite the talk of the town these days."

Columba cocked his head to one side in curiosity. "Water monster?"

"Aye," replied the king. "A great serpent has found its way into the depths of the loch. He ate a fisherman who was casting his nets only a few weeks ago. I didna' see it myself, but I heard it was a terrible sight. Nothing was left of him but the buttons on his shirt! The beast spit them out and swam away."

Columba laughed out loud. "I find that hard to believe, my king. Are you sure someone is not jesting with you?"

"No one would dare tell me false rumors," replied the king indignantly. "The gods foretold of it. My seer predicted an attack from the water. The fishermen now cast their nets from the shore, and some will never set foot in a boat again."

"It is just superstition. There is no such monster in the loch. Your people will starve if they cannot go out and fish. They must have faith and overcome their fear of such nonsense."

Bredai suddenly stood up. In his eyes was a strange look of terror. "Come, Columbkille, down to the docks and speak to the fishermen yourself. They will tell you what they saw!"

Taking one last gulp of his wine, King Bredai led the way, while Columba and the other monks put down their food and followed him down the hill from the fortress, retracing their steps to the water's edge. By now, a crowd of onlookers had gathered near the dock, eager to see what all the fuss was about. They wandered among the fishermen on the shore.

"Tell this man of god aboot the sea monster!" shouted the king into the crowd.

A small man came toward them. He dug in his shirt and produced a handful of buttons. "It is true! This is all that was left of him!"

"Perhaps it was a whale or a dolphin you saw," replied Columba. "I have travelled this loch for years now and have never seen such a beast."

The man shook his head. "No, it was real, I assure you. A fiercer creature I have never seen."

Columba fingered the buttons against the man's palm and glanced around at the wide-eyed stares of the people. Just as he was beginning to speak, someone yelled out, "Look, out in the loch! The beast has returned!"

All eyes shifted. The color of the water near the shore had changed from blue to the shade of whiskey as if the bottom of the loch had been stirred up from the depths. At first there were only swells and bubbles swirling with the river current, lapping against the shore. Then, further out, something moved across from north to south, creating a white wake behind it. Suddenly and without warning, a great serpent-like creature leaped from beneath the water and crashed below again causing a wave to come ashore and splash on the beach. The crowd of people quickly moved away from the water and were cowering on the road into town. The monks turned to Columba in terror.

Columba rubbed his chin. *Perhaps a whale has found its way up the river from the sea*, he thought logically. Whatever it was, whatever mighty beast had invaded the loch, *his* God was mightier.

"Brother Lugne," he said to the monk nearest his side. "You are by far the best swimmer among us. Remove your shoes and bind up your robe and step down into the water to show our faith to the people."

The monk did as he was bid, albeit nervously. He pulled off his shoes and stepped out into the water to his knees. "Is this far enough, Brother Columba?"

"Go deeper still," replied Columba. "Until the water is up to your chin."

The people gawked at what they anticipated would be a human sacrifice before them. The king was watching the monk intently as Brother Lugne sank deeper and deeper, waiting for something to happen. He stopped but remained standing in the cold water of the loch. All the eyes on the shore were upon him. After a few minutes had passed there was another swirling of the water just beyond where the monk stood and then another great splash like the slapping of a fish tail. Out of the water jumped a great black creature with bulging eyes and a long slender body. It immediately dove beneath the surface and came back up again nearer to the monk, blowing bubbles

35

from its nostrils, floating with only his eyes visible above the water. Lugne began to shiver in fear. He closed his eyes in silent prayer. He turned around slowly hoping to escape to shore before he was devoured.

"Stay where you are, Brother. Do not move!" shouted Columba. He walked to the very edge of the water and held up the cross that hung around his neck gripping it tightly in his fingers. "Oh Lord, I beseech you! Protect your disciple from this water beast!" he shouted. Then he pointed beyond Brother Lugne's head and spoke directly to the beast. "Monster of the deep depart these waters! You will not harm a man of God for it is God who created you and it is God who can destroy you at his will!"

Poor Lugne remained frozen up to his shoulders in the water, afraid to look behind him. The creature's eyes that were above the water blinked and then slowly sank below the surface again. Tense moments passed. Then, yards away, out in the loch, the creature slapped its great tail one more time on the surface as it swam away in haste, leaving a wake behind it.

The king was shaking his head in disbelief. The people who had gathered near the dock began murmuring while Lugne waded quickly back to shore. All eyes were on Columba.

"You have truly performed a miracle, my friend," said the king. "Your god has shown his power in such a way he cannae be denied. I am sorry I doubted you."

Columba seized on the opportunity. He took a few steps and stood in the water, motioning for the king to follow him. "Come, Bredai. There is no need to be afraid. God will protect you. Let me baptize you in his name and bless you for all time."

The king snapped out of the spell cast upon him by the strange event. "I dinnae' wish to provoke the gods," he said laughingly. "Come, Columbkille. Let us return to our meal. You will all want to rest after your journey. We still have much to talk aboot."

Disappointed but not deterred, Columba followed while his brothers helped poor Lugne out of the water. Back in the king's home, the other monks retired to their sleep sacks in a corner of the great room. The king's servants gave Lugne a warm blanket while he dried his wet robe near the fire and the king poured his friend more wine. They sat at the great table long into the night, exchanging news. This time it was the king who brought up the subject of faith.

"Will you be sailing back through Loch Ness on your journey home?" he asked when sleep and wine had caused his eyelids to become heavy.

Columba nodded his head.

"May I ask a favor of you then?"

"Of course, my king," replied the monk.

"There is someone I wish you to pay a visit to. There is a fortress at Airchartdan, and a man there named Emchath. He is an old friend of mine and I fear he is dying as we speak. I believe your wise counsel may comfort him."

"Is that the place that sits high on a rock over the water a few miles south of here?"

"Aye, that is the place. Can you stop on your way home and see him? It would mean a lot to me."

"I will be happy to visit your friend and I thank you for your faith in *me* if not in my *God*."

They wandered off to sleep then. At dawn, they broke their fast together before Columba's departure. The king walked with them to the dock and embraced Columba warmly as the monks climbed back aboard their strange vessel. "Safe travels, my friend. Come visit me again in the spring," he said. "And you won't forget your promise?"

"No," replied Columba. "I will not forget."

As they rowed back onto the loch and steered toward the western shore the monks, especially Lugne, were a little nervous after the events of the day before and kept vigil eyes on the surface of the water for signs of the beast returning. The current flowed north, pulled by the River Ness which made their departure more difficult now that they were rowing against the flow, but soon had a sail full of wind to propel them. Weary after a summer of missionary work across the vast wilderness of Scotland they were all eager to return to their monastery on the island of Iona for rest and rejuvenation. There was little conversation among them, all being trained in the art of silence and obedience, but their minds were on alert, wondering when the monster would surface again.

CHAPTER THREE "THE GREAT STORM"

George Urquhart and the others returned after three days laboring in Inverness, digging sewer pits and repairing leaking roofs by day, drinking in a tavern and sleeping their drunkenness off every night in the town livery before the Ceardannan packed up and moved on again. Meanwhile, Annie had taken temporary shelter in the wagon with her new companion, Deidre, until the men returned, and she went back to her bed on the beach. When they came, the men brought food and supplies. The next day a group went hunting in the nearby woods where they managed to shoot a deer so there was a spit-roasted haunch that night for supper. It was grand, eating like kings and queens around a roaring campfire and Annie ate until her stomach ached. After helping Deidre with the supper dishes, she found herself a spot of soft sand and bedded herself down. Alex found her and again camped at her feet with George and Angus a few yards away.

Once they were on the road again, Annie's mood began to change slowly for the better. For the first time since they had joined the Ceardannan she felt like she had made a friend in Deidre and a motherly bond had developed between them. She walked along beside Alex today with almost a skip in her step. The fresh air in her lungs, the blue sky above and the warmth of the sun overhead seemed to make life bearable again. Her father and Angus stuck close to Geoffrey at the front of the caravan. It was a political move, one she understood. George Urquhart was a natural born salesman, and he was determined to rise in the Ceardannan. A friendship with the leader of the clan was his assurance of future work.

The road followed the loch for a good distance until it entered a thick wood, and the sun went away, only flashing occasionally from between the treetops. The air became still with no breeze to sweep away the dank odor of rotting soil and leaves. When they finally stopped for the night, content with a full belly of leftover venison and the security of her faithful brother nearby, Annie closed her eyes and waited for sleep to come. Soon the wind picked up and made a strange moaning sound as it thrashed through the trees. In the darkness an owl hooted as the voices of the gypsies died down to murmurs and snoring. Somewhere in the wee hours, it began to rain. Annie felt warm, wet droplets on her face, and she burrowed deeper beneath her blanket. Soon, the rain became a deluge, and she awoke to the sounds of others scurrying around the camp, taking cover beneath the wagons and awnings. Alex awakened and together they sought out a protected place further into the woods to keep dry. By then the wind had grown from a moan to an ear-piercing whistle and the trees were bending, scraping their branches together. For hours it whipped away at the wagon covers and tents while, huddled together, the Ceardannan waited it out, clutching desperately to everything they owned.

By morning, the entire campground was submerged. The wagon that carried the newly purchased food was ankle-deep in rainwater; the bags of flour and much of the other food was ruined. Annie got up and went to help Deidre and the others try to salvage what they could. All the wagons were up righted and drained. Others went out to search for belongings that had been blown away.

"We can get replacements in Drumnadrochit up ahead," Geoffrey told them, not at all worried. "After a storm like this there will be work aplenty!"

All that day the women spread their linens and spare clothing on ropes strung across the camp to dry while they cooked up all the food that would most certainly spoil if not used. Wagon covers that were torn were mended and the men celebrated their survival over the storm with music and whiskey, although the wet bagpipe now honked like a goose, and the fiddle's strings twanged flat against the damp wood. After finishing her assigned chores, Annie found herself wandering in the woods out of boredom, not searching for anything, only biding time until they moved on again. She gathered clumps of grass which she brought back for the wizard's horse. Some of the wagons had to be pulled out of the mud, but by late afternoon they were on their way again. For miles, they trudged ahead through the soggy forest.

Annie ran ahead of the caravan when they finally emerged from the shadows of the trees. At the bottom of the hill, before the road rose sharply upward to the west, she saw the old, abandoned castle for the first time, sitting precariously at the edge of the loch on a jagged, rocky cliff separated from them by a deep ravine that had filled with rushing rainwater. There was a rumble of excitement at the sight. Before them, the men of the Ceardannan saw the storm-ravaged tower and walls as a bounty of usable stone and lumber ripe for the picking. As soon as they had circled the wagons and unhitched the horses, they all began to push past Annie in their greed, swarming across a narrow rock bridge with empty gunny sacks to collect their loot. Annie watched them disappear behind the rock walls, sensing something different about the castle; something told her it was far more special than a mere heap of stone. She could not explain it. She felt a strange, spiritual connection to the old ruin, much the way she had felt back in Cromarty when she leaned her back against the castle walls. Why, she did not know, but the hair stood up on the nape of her neck and her stomach quivered when she looked at it.

41

And, for the first time in her life, she was going to see a castle on the *inside*!

It was cold on the ground and damp from the previous night's storm, and Annie might as well have been barefoot for her shoes were quickly soaked through from the wet grass. She reached the bridge and slowed her pace to walk across the rough, wet cobbles. While the men rushed ahead to pick the castle clean, she briefly stopped to peer over the side, at the river flowing underneath her and out into the loch. She watched a family of fat, round toads huddling on the bank to avoid being swept away in the current of the swollen creek. Toads and other creatures intrigued her since the time she had raised a gaggle of tadpoles in a jar back in Cromarty until her father had insisted that she dump them in the firth. "Toads are not pets!" he had scolded her. "We'll find you a dog," he told her, but the dog never materialized. It was just as well; the Urquharts did not need another hungry mouth to feed. She looked back toward the camp and saw the wizard drawing a hatful of water from the creek to take to his horse. She had nicknamed the horse Bobbin because the wheels on the wizard's wagon reminded her of her mother's spinning bobbins which she remembered playing with as a wee bairn. She felt pity for the decrepit old animal, having to lug heavy loads every day, in good weather and bad. She smiled now at the sight of the horse straining against its yoke to steal bites of wet grass. The horse was becoming as close to a pet as she would ever have.

She lingered on the bridge, running her hands over the railing, feeling the patterns of the wood and the roughness of the stone pillars with her fingertips when suddenly she felt a strange tremor tickling her palms and the soles of her feet, as if the bridge was moving beneath her. Her arms rippled with gooseflesh, and she shivered from the sensation. Looking up, toward the crumbling walls of the old castle, she felt forcefully drawn in, as if from some invisible spirit. *Did no one else feel it?* she wondered doubtfully. She looked back at the people of the Ceardannan. *Probably not*, as the women were busy setting up camp and all the men seemed to care about was plundering the spoils.

After a few moments, she moved forward, passing over the bridge and under the rusted teeth of the portcullis that snarled down at her. All that was left of a burned gatehouse was now a soggy, blackened mire of wood and stone. The storm was obviously not the first attack the castle had suffered. From the looks of it, it had weathered many military battles before the storm had struck the final blow. There were visible gashes in the walls from heavy artillery fire. The men spread out across the nether bailey, trampling the blades of grass that were still lying limp from the rain, startling the deer grazing there into bolting up the hills to higher ground. Annie stayed in the shadows of the interior wall, feeling the coolness of the stone against her palms. As the men mulled about, filling their sacks with anything usable for trade, she took in the courtyard around her with fascination.

The interior buildings had succumbed to decay also, roofless and crumbling, the remaining stones white and permanently etched in bird droppings. Weeds now choked out what was once a vegetable garden and the stones of an old dovecot had toppled from the storm, its nests empty, its feathered residents long since flown. The only structures left untouched by weather and war were two unmarked standing stones on a grassy slope. For a moment, she stood staring at them in wonder before she finally caught up with George and her brothers.

"Seems odd that there's no one else out to scavenge," she heard Angus tell their father.

George Urquhart shrugged. "It's because we got here first," he said, already filling his bag with shiny, wet stones. "And a bounty has been laid out before us, stupid boy! Pry loose those latches and braces over there where the wood is burned. Save the boards that are not charred too badly. And get to it before we *do* have competition from others."

No wonder Angus never spoke, she thought to herself. Her father never had anything nice to say to him or any of his children.

While the men of the Ceardannan rifled through the ruins of the castle, gleaning anything that was of value, Annie wandered off unnoticed to explore the rest of the courtyard. *Why would the high lairds who owned this castle have abandoned such a wonderful place*? she wondered. She remembered the castle in Cromarty that was now occupied by English usurpers. How tall and regal it stood above the town, how she had for years longed to see beyond its gates. While this castle was not *her* castle she was *on* the inside! *This castle must have had its day too*, she thought dreamily. It must have been quite a sight on the edge of the loch, like a proud sentry watching over all the ships that passed by before it had crumbled and fallen into disrepair. She couldn't help but wonder if it had been stolen from another family like hers. Now, it seemed that no one wanted it except the Ceardannan who only wanted to plunder and destroy its remains.

The condition of the castle didn't really surprise her. Between the Jacobites and the English soldiers who were battling all over Scotland, armies were laying waste to everything. She never really understood the reasons. From conversations she had overheard her brothers have, Scotland had been fighting for its independence for many centuries and England was just not willing to let it go. And, to make matters worse, the Scottish clans fought amongst themselves, so they never really presented a united front. It was no wonder they couldn't win the war. They couldn't even stand together for the sake of Scotland. Back in Cromarty, some still wore their clan "colors" proudly while others put them away for a better time. After the fall of their own clan, her father had closeted his, more from shame than politics. Personally, she didn't see what all the fuss was about; she didn't care if it were a Protestant or a Catholic king in England. She had not been in a church since her baptism. She knew from an old rosary that her mother had been Catholic, and she had seen her brother Alex cross himself once when a funeral procession passed by. She herself had no particular religious faith, only a desire to see peace in Scotland and an end to the wars.

She continued to circle the courtyard near what was left of the outer wall, touching the rough stones with her fingertips as she walked along. Still damp from the rain, they shone bright and clean in the sun that now hovered overhead. Birds sat atop the wall, spying earthworms popping up from the saturated soil and flew over her now and then to pluck them from the soft earth. She found her way through the now-roofless buildings, one large one that might have been a grand hall and another smaller one that appeared to be the castle kitchen. An old cutting board, now warped and falling apart, lay submerged in rainwater and there was the remnant of an old fireplace, still dripping blackened tears onto the floor. In another enclosure she found horse droppings floating in a wide puddle like apples for bobbing at a town faire and mildewed straw strewn about suggesting it had been a stable. Another tiny building, roofless as well, had a Celtic cross etched in the stone, possibly an old chapel. She found furrowed rows of soil, half-submerged in water, with tiny carrot leaves poking up and she pulled one up, rinsing it in the puddle before she sank her teeth into it. It was still sweet, yet misshapen, and it tasted fine. Annie chewed it down to its tiny green leaves. She then pulled up two more and tucked them under the waistband of her skirt to take back to Bobbin.

Above the rear of the courtyard, she nearly stepped off a sheer cliff where the pathway ended abruptly at what must have been a stairway leading down to the water's edge. She caught herself and looked down on the beach. There was nothing left but a steep, muddy bank, impossible to descend without falling. At the bottom of the hill lay an array of stones from the washed-away steps, now haphazardly strewn across the beach. Annie stared at the water lapping against the shore, noticing for the first time how the color of it had changed. No longer was it blue and serene as it had looked the first time she had set eyes upon it back in Inverness. Now, the water looked unsettled, swirling, and gurgling and spitting foam against the rocks. It was murky and dull, the color of the whiskey her father drank.

She heard her name being called. It was Alex' voice and she turned just as he came up behind her, lugging a heavy sack over his shoulder.

"Are you quite finished exploring?" he asked. "I have to go help load this stuff into the wagons. You'd better come along. I dinnae' want you falling over a cliff or anything."

"Alex, I am quite capable of taking care of myself."

"Ya, I know, but come along anyway, so I won't havta' worry aboot you."

Annie followed him back across the grassy knoll and stopped just for a moment to look up at the tower. "Tomorra' I will see what's inside that tower," she said, grinning. Maybe Angus was right. Maybe it *would* be an adventure after all.

CHAPTER FOUR "EMCHATH"

Grateful for the wind that provided them swift passage, Columba and the other monks stepped out of the currach on the sand beneath the rocky promontory known to locals as Airchartdan and immediately fell to their knees in prayer. God had seen to it that the creature that made Loch Ness its home had not hindered their voyage. Lugne, was especially pleased that the beast had not resurfaced.

Their reception was not as cordial as the one they had received back in Inverness. Three armed and savage-looking men, naked and painted to the waist came running down a steep incline of rock and earthen steps to confront them and inquire about their identity. Columba smiled calmly at them and spoke to them in Pictish. "I have come from the home of King Bredai with a message for your chieftain." The expressions on the faces of the men remained suspicious so Columba continued. "Bredai is concerned for the health of Emchath, his friend. He bade me to visit and give what comfort I can to him."

Hearing their native tongue spoken, the men accepted them and escorted the line of brown-cloaked monks up the narrow stair. At the top they were greeted with more stares and mouths agog as they passed by, men and women and children with painted skin in various stages of undress. There was no warm welcome as there had been with King Bredai. This time they were led into a wooden fortress of darkened gloom and a house made of rough-hewn logs and sod. It was a large room, the center of which was an open hearth of stone. "My brothers will remain here whilst I visit with your chieftain," Columba told the three men and followed them into Emchath's bedchamber as the other monks sat down around the hearth to wait.

Inside the smaller room it was even darker than the main hall; there was but one narrow window to let in a sliver of sunlight. Emchath was lying on a pile of straw mattresses, covered with a thin sheet that smelled of perspiration. His face was tired and pale, and he looked up at his guest with the dull unresponsive eyes of a soon-to-be corpse.

"I have come from the court of Bredai," Columba said softly as he approached the bed and took the old man's hand in his. "I am Columbkille from the Isle of Iona. I have been a friend of the king for many years now. He wanted me to come and give you blessings from my god in this your hour of sickness."

Emchath was weak but he tried to squeeze Columba's hand, falling back against his pillow from the exertion. "Bredai and I fought together in many battles," he whispered, his voice rising from his chest like a death rattle. "Any friend of his is a friend of mine."

Columba spotted a three-legged stool nearby and pulled it close to the bedside. "How can I be of comfort to you, Sir? May I pray with you for healing and the restoration of your health?"

Emchath shook his head. "My health is sadly beyond prayer," he said, "but I will take blessings from any and all the gods, if they choose to give them."

A moment of silent prayer ensued. Columba smiled. "I have passed your magnificent fortress many times and have wondered what mighty king lived here. I am pleased to know you. Can I do anything else to comfort you? Bring you food or drink? Read to you from the holy scriptures?"

"No, but thank ye," said Emchath. "Tell me how you know of king Bredai? Your tongue doesna' have the accent of a Pict and you certainly dinnae' dress like one."

"You are correct," replied Columba, "my family roots are in Ireland. King Bredai tells me *your* ancestors came from Ulster as well. I have a monastery on the Isle of Iona off the coast of Dal Riata. We are returning home now, but the king was worried about your welfare, and I promised him I would look in on you."

Emchath suddenly broke into a horrible spasm of coughing and there was a lull in the conversation. A bare-breasted woman hurried into the room and poured water from a bedside pitcher which she held up to his lips. Embarrassed, Columba looked away. Some of the Pictish customs were hard for him to embrace; open nakedness was one of them. After he had wet his throat, the old man closed his eyes from exhaustion and the woman left the room. When he could talk again, he asked the same questions that Bredai had asked, about war coming up from the south. Again, Columba reassured him that he had seen no signs of pending military action.

"There is always war coming from south of the wall," replied Emchath. "They will never leave us in peace. Tell me, Monk, what is there in our rocky highlands that they want so badly?"

"Who knows what they want?" said Columba. "Greed and power are diseases that infect most men, and it eventually leads to their downfall. You needn't worry, though. You have the perfect vantage point from which to see up and down the loch. If they *do* come you will not be caught by surprise."

"We just want to be left alone."

Columba removed the cross from around his neck and placed it in Emchath's hand. "Let me bless you with the peace you long for, Sir. My god is a powerful and faithful god. Allow me to bring you into his light and protection."

The old man nodded, and Columba recited a baptismal prayer.

He then reached for the cup of water at the bedside and with his fingers dabbled droplets across the dying man's chest. "I baptize you in the name of the Father, the Son and the Holy Spirit."

Emotion always gripped Columba after he had performed a baptism. He paused to catch his breath and feel God's presence. *One more pagan he had saved from eternal damnation*.

"Is there anything you wish to confess, Sir? Sins you wish to be forgiven for?"

Emchath's eyes lowered, and a strange sadness came over his wrinkled face. "I have killed many men but not for the sport of it. Only to protect what is mine."

"Then you shall surely be forgiven."

"I have not always been kind to my wife. I have beat her on occasion."

"That can be forgiven also if you recognize your sin and repent and do not repeat it."

A raspy laugh emitted from Emchath's throat. "In my condition? That is not likely!"

He fell back against his pillow again, spent from too much conversation.

The once powerful chieftain of Airchartdan then expired, his chest expanding and then collapsing silently and peacefully as his entire body went limp. Columba whispered a final prayer over him and left the wooden crucifix in Emchath's dead hands to take with him into the afterlife.

They buried him in the courtyard three days later beneath a great mound of earth, Columba presiding over the funeral. All the Pictish chieftains came from miles around, including King Bredai, who arrived on his long ship decked out as a royal barge. A slab of granite was split from the cliffs on the promontory and hauled up to be placed upon his grave. In the years to follow, the red deer began to come down from the hills; the does with their speckled fawns, the young bucks in their velvet, and even the grand stags from the highest peaks would come to rest in its shade or bask in the warmth of the sun reflected on the stone.

Bredai and Columba did not know it then, but it would be the last time they would see one another, for both would die shortly after, the king in his fortress in Inverness and the monk in his monastery on Iona.

CHAPTER FIVE "WOMAN IN THE STAIRWELL"

There was much jubilation that night around the Ceardannan campfire and George Urquhart got quite drunk, so much so that his sons literally had to carry him back to his bed sack unconscious. Annie's disgust was only tempered by the anticipation of exploring more of the castle the next day and after she had helped Diedre with the supper chores, she once again wandered off to her own bed on the bank of the rain-filled moat. It was a pleasant night with the croaking of the toads and the rushing of the water in her ears. The sky had cleared. Gone were the rainclouds and only stars remained, twinkling down at her as her eyelids began to grow heavy. In the distance she could see the great tower standing above the castle battlements, now only a black shadow against the pale night sky.

When morning came, the men were up early and eager to attack the old castle again. It amused her to see her father holding his aching head in his hands, suffering from a nasty hangover. *Serves him right*, she thought haughtily. She exchanged knowing smiles with Alex. As they started down the hill toward the castle, a stranger met them on the road: a tall, lanky man with a shepherds' staff guiding a half dozen rangy sheep. He eyed the sacks slung over their shoulders and the previous day's bounty: the wagons piled high with the broken stone and wood.

"G'wine to plunder the old castle, are ye?" he asked with a slight raise of his eyebrows.

Geoffrey came forward to greet him. "Tis not against the law, is it? The storm brought the walls down. Cannae' blame no one but *God* for that."

The shepherd shrugged. "I guess it's not a crime. But beware of the spirits within those walls. Many's the man who has tried to do the same. They're all under the ground now. Have you not wondered why none of the locals are down here challenging you for all this good stone?"

The conversation piqued the interest of several others, including Alex and Angus. "Spirits? What sort of spirits?"

"Why the spirits of the loch," replied the shepherd. "The Druids have congregated in the old castle for centuries. That's why it has been abandoned. No sane man would steal from the Druids and risk their wrath."

George's face squinted. "Ah, superstition! There's nothing there but broken stones and burned wood. Nothing to be afraid of."

Alex was not so sure. "*Druids*, you say? Have you seen them yourself?"

"They only come at night. Ye can see their torches from up the hill. Dancing in circles and singing their songs. Witches. Druids. Whatever you want to call them. Ya wouldna' find me camped anywhere near this place when the full moon comes out. Just be careful, that's all I'm sayin'."

With that he prodded his sheep on down the road leaving Geoffrey and the others to contemplate his warning. George laughed out loud. "Dinnae' be concerned, Men. He is just an old man who likes to tell stories. We'll make a fine living with the goods we reap from this place."

Annie noticed the wizard working his way into the group, his tall hat spiking up above the others' heads. He had a worried look on his face. "The shepherd may be old but he's not crazy," he said to Geoffrey. "Dinnae' confuse the Druids with the faeries of the glen. They are *real*! And they dinnae' just steal your bread and ale when you are asleep. They can cast powerful spells. You boys can do what you want. *I'll* not be stealin' from them." He turned and walked away, back to his wagon where Bobbin was sleeping in the grass.

Annie smiled at the wizard and his superstitions.

"Poor old Olin," remarked George. "He is a relic from the past. He still believes in the faerie stories his mum told him."

There was laughter after that, but Annie sensed it was guarded. It wasn't only the old who were leery of witches and the powers of the dark side. She herself was a bit apprehensive but her curiosity was stronger than her fear. She was even more determined to get back inside that castle. And she had learned the wizard's name. As difficult as it had been for her to draw him into conversations, he had allowed her to feed his horse grass and tubers and she was beginning to become fond of the old curmudgeon. She had developed affection for Deidre as well and even Geoffrey, gruff as his demeanor was. Her original suspicion of the Ceardannan had been softened by the discovery that they were not much different than the poor townsfolk back in Cromarty. They were hard-working, hard-drinking men and women who minded their own business and didn't stick their noses into others' affairs. Living among them was not as bad as she had anticipated although she would never admit it to her family.

The dawn was bright against a brilliant blue sky, and it glistened off the flecks in the granite stones of the castle. Her father and brothers were helping Geoffrey and the others pull two wagons closer to the bridge to make loading them easier. They had rigged ropes and horses to pull the heavy rocks from the courtyard. Annie paid a visit to the wizard and his horse before she set out on her adventure for the day.

"Good Morrow, Olin," she said pleasantly.

The old man was sitting on the grass beside his wagon, cross-legged, his fingers deftly weaving a new basket from dried reeds. He looked up at her, surprised. She had never called him by name before.

"So ye think we are *friends* now, do ya? Just because you know my name?"

"No, Sir," replied Annie. "But I should like to be. I think I have already made friends with your horse. Does he have a name as well?"

The wizard chuckled. "Horses dinnae' need no name. He's an animal, a beast of burden, that's all. Where *do* you get your silly notions, Lassie?"

"My name is not Lassie, it's Annie. And I have given a name to your horse. I call him Bobbin. The wheels on your wagon remind me of the bobbins on my mum's spinning wheel."

"Bobbin, is it? Well, dinnae' get any ideas. He is no riding horse, so dinnae' ask. He's meant for pulling a wagon, not fer ladies' sport."

Annie could see through his gruff exterior and spotted a laughing twinkle in his eye.

"Well, I will not bother you further, Sir. I am going exploring in the castle today."

The wizard gave her an ominous look. "Be careful, Lassie. There's something strange aboot that place."

55

"Why must you always be so superstitious?"

"Didna' ya see the light in the tower last night?"

Annie shook her head.

"Well, just be careful, that's all."

She pulled the carrots tucked in her skirt for Bobbin and rubbed his ears.

The castle was calling to her. She could hear its voice on the wind. As she passed over the bridge, she noticed the water level had receded, leaving the fat toads more room on the muddy bank where they were sunning themselves. A few wood ducks had appeared on the bank too, sharing the dawn's warmth with them. All seemed serene in the morning air. Annie could not help thinking about Olin's words…. had he truly seen a light in the tower? Was there some ghostly being there? As she passed through the ruined gatehouse, she stared up at the remains of the five-story monolith, its gaping wounds staring back at her. She started toward it, her feet swishing through the tall grass. A drapery ballooned out from the third story and flapped noisily on the wind above her head. Was it saying *stay back, Girl?* Or beckoning her to come inside? At that point, Annie did not care. Superstition or not she was determined to explore!

Suddenly, she was surrounded by the men gathering stones. She heard her father behind her.

"Out of the way, Annie! The men cannae' be tripping over you all day. Go back to camp and find yerself something useful to do."

Alex and Angus followed her father. Alex smiled at her. "You can gather the small stones, Annie, if'n you want to help. But, over there, out of the way. You might stumble on the larger ones."

George grumbled and hoisted his gunny sack over his shoulder. "Well, just do it somewhere else. Not under our feet." He pushed her aside. Annie backed away and wandered toward the washed-out stairway that led down to the water, disappointed at being kept from the tower. The mud had dried somewhat, and she managed to skate down on her feet without getting anything dirty except her shoes. At the bottom of the hill, she had a surprise. The stones that had fallen in the storm, which had been haphazardly strewn across the beach only the afternoon before, were now neatly stacked in a row, in perfect formation, like the burial cairns in the cemetery back in Cromarty. She stepped forward and touched them, wondering who had taken the time to stack them with such precision, the large ones as a foundation, gradually getting smaller up to the tiny pebbles at the top. She was standing in the shadow of the tower, and she looked up at the narrow slits that were the windows. Was the person who had done this up there watching her? She felt invisible eyes upon her. Almost afraid she would lock glances with what the shepherd called a Druid, she put her head down and walked on, leaving the standing stones. Picking up a stick she began drawing in the wet sand, doodling, passing the time. After a few yards, she stepped out of the shadow of the tower and into the sunlight again. She collected a few shells, tying them up in her apron and paused to watch a dragon-fly dancing on the surface of the water.

Annie wandered a long way down the shore, ducking underneath the drooping branches of the wych elms that leaned out over the water. Thinking she could not get lost if she stayed near the shore and would find her way back to the castle, she walked for over an hour, until the sun had risen high in the sky and finally found a flat rock to sit and rest before she turned back. The rock was warm against her shoulders, and she felt her cheeks begin to burn slightly. She dawdled, thinking about the strange standing stones, wondering if Druids and witches really existed in the world. She would speak to Olin about it. He seemed to know all about Druids.

She started back toward the castle, taking off her shoes and treading softly over the smooth stones. As she neared the collapsed stairwell, she felt it again…. the familiar tremor in the ground beneath her feet. She shivered slightly and looked up at the tower, the sun now behind it, the shadows from it stretching out over the water like an awning. When she began the climb up the steep bank, Alex appeared at the top, looking down at her, smiling.

"We are going back to the camp to get something to eat, Annie. Want to come?"

Annie's mind raced. Here was the opportunity to explore the tower without being underfoot. "Nah," she replied. "I'm not hungry. I just want to wander around." She looked down at the beach and pointed to the standing stones. "Look, Alex, what someone has done with the stones! Who woulda' done it?"

Alex' eyes narrowed, and he took in the sight of the carefully stacked stone towers. "I dunno, Annie. Maybe the Druids." He laughed then and reached out to help her up the bank.

"Do you believe there *is* such a thing?"

"Nah," he replied. "Just superstition. You just take care you dinnae' fall and hurt yerself, climbing among the rocks like a mountain goat."

"I'll be fine."

He left her then, standing at the top of the cliff, and Annie's eyes took in the entire rolling courtyard, now empty and green and peaceful without the intrusion of the Ceardannan. Many of the fallen stones had been removed, hauled off to the wagons; a stack of wood sat near the gatehouse ready to be carried out. They'd left nothing behind in the courtyard, stripping the place down to its bare nakedness. She wondered what they had left behind in the tower as she hurried forward and entered the open doorway into a small room with a hearth at one end. The floor was covered in dust; the footprints of the men and a trail of rat droppings led to gaps in the crumbling walls. Half the stones above the firepit had been torn loose, leaving pockets of yellowed mortar, giving it the appearance of a face with missing teeth. Nothing to see here, she moved onward and upward.

It was a precipitous climb up the circular stairwell and so narrow it brushed her shoulders. The steps were so steep and close together she used her hands to guide herself up to the next, vertically crawling. Up, up, up she went, watching the glimmer of sunlight from the open roof above her as it spiraled down the walls, lighting her path. The air smelled damp and musty from the rain on the aged stones. She came to another doorway, a room even smaller than the one below it. Another toothless fireplace sharing the same chimney as the ground floor. Walking across the dusty footprints left by the men of the Ceardannan she leaned into the blackened firebox and shouted up the empty shaft. "Druids! Are you there?" The echo of her own voice in the chamber startled her. She stepped back and laughed at herself. An old drapery moved eerily in the breeze coming through a single open window. She reached out and put her hands on it, the fabric faded and stiff and soiled now, smelling of mildew and rot. *Who had slept here*, she wondered? *The lairds of the castle? Visiting kings, perhaps? Maybe Robert the Bruce or even William Wallace?*

The stairwell beckoned her again and she climbed even higher, finally stepping out onto the creneled battlement at the very pinnacle of the tower. Below her, the loch stretched out endlessly at her feet. The wind circled around her, stirring the dust and mortar from the crumbled stones, disheveling her hair and billowing her skirt. She looked back toward the camp and could see the campfire burning and the men gathered around it. She waved, not knowing if anyone could see her. Then she turned back to the loch and the breathtaking view.

With nothing new to see she started downward again, descending the spiraling stair, holding her skirt high to keep from tripping and tumbling over her own feet. Down, down, down she went to the ground floor where she discovered yet another narrow staircase leading below into a dungeon. This one was dark, with no sunlight to guide her, lit only with a single horsehair torch bracketed to the wall. Removing it from the wall, she held it high above her head. It got darker the deeper she went, and she balanced herself against the walls for support. At the bottom was a wide room once used for storage with rotten casks and broken crates strewn about, lit only with the glow of the torch. She circled the outer wall touching the cold stones, smelling the mustiness of centuries between them. It was then she heard rushing water below her and came across an old iron grate on the floor, rusted with age. As she crouched down to peer through the tiny square openings, she smelled the dank mist rising from the water below. *A place for bathing?* she wondered, *or the castle sewer?* An old, corroded padlock was clasped around a latch holding the grate closed, preventing her from exploring further. She stood up, brushing the smudges of rust off her skirt and hands, and turned around to leave.

There, standing above her in the open stairwell, was an old woman, tiny and frail looking, with steel-grey hair pulled tightly against her temples and knotted at the nape of her neck. Her skin was gossamer-thin, with fat, purple veins crawling across the back of her white hands like earthworms. She wore a long white dress that dragged the floor and was barefooted; her calloused and dusty toes stuck out obscenely from beneath her skirt. Although she did not smile at Annie, there was a strange benevolence in her face. It was a wise face, creased with years of toil and hardship, no doubt. She did not know what a Druid should look like, or if the old woman was just an ordinary, commonplace witch but, somehow, she did not feel afraid of this stranger. She opened her mouth to speak but in an instant the woman had disappeared up the darkened stairwell. She gripped the torch tightly and ran up the steps after her. When she reached the ground floor and looked out on the empty courtyard, the strange woman had vanished as if she had never been there.

CHAPTER SIX "BATTLE WITH THE BOAR"

AnCuMor ran ahead of the horses, a massive Irish wolfhound with a tangled coat the color of burnt ash, and large eyes as black as peat. His master, Conachar Mor, leading a small army of fifty men on horseback, followed, resting at Fort Augustus overnight before they galloped northward along the western shore of Loch Ness. The dog had never set foot on Scottish soil before and yet he seemed to know the way to Airchartdan instinctively. He stopped only intermittently to flush a bird from the undergrowth or to lift his leg and piss on a tree, marking his territory, leaving his wet signature to warn anyone who followed.

"Stupid dog," Conachar mumbled under his breath, "Fouls everything he passes."

The dog was a constant irritation to him, always leaving his coarse hair on his clothing and bedding, slobbering incessantly whenever there was food nearby. He had never encouraged the unpleasant animal to accompany him, a mongrel pup who had been whelped in the castle stable, but the dog had become loyal nevertheless, sticking to Conachar's side, growling at strangers who approached his master. He had happily followed the soldiers and horses out of Ulster, across on the boat and onto Scottish soil. Now he took the lead instinctively as if he were guiding the men.

Conachar Mor had come to fight alongside Malcom III to avenge the murder of the king, Malcom's own father, by Macbeth, the usurper who now wore the Scottish crown. The royal house of Ulster had long supported the Scottish kings in their wars against the English. Now it was an internal struggle that was tearing Scotland apart. After the death of King Duncan, his wife and her two young sons, Malcom and Donald Bane, had fled Scotland in fear that their lives were in danger too. Malcom had now returned from exile as an adult, with the support of the English king Edward the Confessor and his armies, to recapture the throne that he believed was his by inheritance. Feeling a little uncomfortable with the English now on their side, Conachar still did not abandon the rightful heir. He vowed to fight alongside Malcom and his armies even if he had to trust the Redcoats.

Conachar was a small, sturdy man, narrow in the hip but robust and stout in the chest. He had a ruddy complexion and an outgoing, jovial nature that put men at ease and encouraged them to trust him. Back in Ireland, women found him a wee bit comical because of his short stature and his red face. Still unmarried, he secretly hoped to entice a Pictish woman into his bed who did not share the snobbishness of the high-born women at home. His family had now all migrated to Scotland, the land of the Picts. The fortress on Loch Ness had been under the control of his kin for centuries ever since his ancestor Emchath had built the first wooden house situated on the great rock over the water.

When they reached the hills above Airchartdan and stopped to look down upon the walls running along the shore of the loch, they were pleased at the sight of hundreds of tethered horses grazing in the grassy meadow.

"Malcom has waited for us to arrive!" shouted Conachar as he kicked his horse and galloped down toward the bridge that spanned the dry moat. The gate was opened, but not for them; they were pushed aside by a hunting party marching out of the courtyard, spears in hand, knives and daggers on their hips. Conachar and his men stopped short and stepped aside to let them pass. The man in the lead leaned down to pet AnCuMor's scruffy head.

Conachar did not know Malcom by sight, only by letters he had received back in Ireland requesting support. He scanned the group of men before him, looking for some recognition that he had been expected and was welcome.

"You are Conachar?" asked the man. "I recognize your standard." He looked down and patted the dog's head again. "I heard that you travelled with a dog for protection."

Conachar laughed. "Him? He can hardly fight the fleas on his back! But, aye, I am Conachar, son of Aoidh. You must be Malcom Canmore. I am pleased to meet you, M'Lord, and honored to ride with you."

Malcom was everything Conachar had expected him to be. Tall And handsome, the picture of a great soldier; his face was ruddy like his own and his eyes were startlingly clear and blue. Conachar alighted from his horse and extended an arm to the son of the rightful King Duncan who had been slain by the usurper. "We welcome you to join us. At the moment we are hungry and going on a boar hunt. Have the grooms stable your horses and come with us." He looked around. "We have extra spears if you have none."

Indeed, Conachar and his men had brought their swords and shields for battle but had not thought to bring hunting weapons. "Aye, my Lord, we will join you!"

A dozen young boys immediately appeared on the bridge and led Conachar's horses off to the courtyard stables while others brought spears. By the time they had armed themselves, Malcom and his men had already marched down the road and entered the woods, disappearing under a canopy of rowan trees. They broke into a jog to catch up with the others.

AnCuMor was panting with excitement jogging at Conachar's side as always.

The forest was deep and dark and silent as the horde of men marched into it. The path underneath their feet was soft and the sound of their boots was muffled; only their breathing and the panting of AnCuMor could be heard among the trees. Birds fluttered upward and small animals scattered through the brush to escape the hunters, away from the death that they recognized in the flash of their steel weapons. But this was no rabbit hunt today. Today the object was the great hairy beast who made its home in the great glen, whose tusks were razor-sharp and whose ferocity knew no bounds. Today they were seeking a more worthy opponent than rabbits or squirrels. The hunting party would be equally matched, even with fifty spears.

For many yards, almost a half mile, they forged ahead, scraping the brush alongside the path to root out the boar. AnCuMor was on alert; the hair on his back standing up like a stiff bristle brush. Sniffing, he crashed in and out of the bushes and tangled roots only to return empty handed to Conachar who had caught up to Malcom and was now walking at his side. "See what I mean? That dog couldna' find a tick with both paws!"

Malcom shook his head. "But he seems like a very loyal pet. If his nose leads us to the boar, he will earn a slice of pork for his supper!"

At that very moment the brush parted ahead of the hunting party. Out of the tangle appeared a huge hairy animal the likes of which Conachar had never seen. It had black eyes and a long whiskered snout from which two enormous tusks protruded, yellowed with age and honed from wear. Immediately the boar lunged forward toward the men. Spears flashed. Some of the men darted for cover in the underbrush. Conachar was glad they were not on horseback. The beast would have cut his horse's legs to ribbons. Unafraid, the boar went on the attack, swinging his long head back and forth, slicing at the men. Two fell to the ground, mortally wounded. Others ran in the opposite direction. Malcom himself was shaken and allowed his men to position themselves between him and the enemy, spears posed and ready, as they had been trained to do in battle.

The moment AnCuMor saw the boar coming toward his master he raced in between them and took hold of the animal's thick neck, shaking it in his mouth. In one swift move, the boar threw his neck sideways, lurching the dog off into the dirt, and turned back toward Conachar. AnCuMor shook it off, blood spittle spraying from his snarling teeth and ran back to engage it, now struggling at the tip of Conachar's spear. This time the dog bit into an eye, his muzzle covered in blood as his teeth found their mark. The boar broke loose of the spear and lunged toward him, ripping into his leg. Conachar was thrown to the ground wounded. It again turned on the dog. With one violent stab, his tusks found their way into the dog's chest. AnCuMor squealed and fell to the ground as Conachar limped forward with his spear, this time planting it deep into the boar's side. The animal collapsed, gasping for its last breath, landing beside the body of AnCuMor. A rousing cheer went up among the men.

They carried Conachar and the other wounded men back to the fortress along with the carcass of the great boar, where they all gathered in the great hall. The cook and the housekeeper nursed Conachar's wounded leg and made him comfortable. Malcom himself poured him a tankard of ale, slapping him on the shoulder. "Fine sportsmanship," he proclaimed as he sat down beside him. "Too bad your hound had to pay the price with his life."

"He was always such a pest. I suppose I will have to be grateful to the mangy beast now."

"Aye," replied Malcom. "He was loyal to the very end."

To save face, Conachar whispered to one of his men. "Go into the woods and bury the damned dog. Lay him deep beneath the stones so the wolves will not dig him up."

They relaxed then, nursing the wounded men, gutting the boar and bringing in a great spit on which to cook it. Conachar and Malcom sat side by side, drinking and laughing until the food was ready and they settled down to eat.

"How long do you intend to stay on here at Airchartdan?" Conachar asked, hoping his leg would have time to heal before the army moved on.

The prince shook his head sadly. "Tonight is the last night, I am afraid. Tomorrow we ride for Northumberland to take on more men. Then, it will be off to challenge Macbeth and war."

Conachar's heart fell. He had come hundreds of miles to fight with this man, to avenge the murder of King Duncan. He looked down at his leg, now wrapped in a bloody bandage. *Cursed dog*, he thought sourly. *He should have let the boar kill me to avoid this shame.*

"I can still ride, M'Lord. Surely you will need all the able-bodied men to support you! This leg will heal; I am sure of it. It is but a scratch!"

Malcom shook his head. "No, I would not feel right leading you into battle when you are already wounded. It is one thing to hobble around the courtyard. Riding hundreds of miles with an injured leg is another matter. It is best you stay here and rest."

Conachar attempted to stand. He foundered and fell back into his chair. He could feel the tears of disappointment well in his eyes. "I'll be fine, Sir. I promise I will not slow you down..."

Malcom rose and placed his hand on Conachar's shoulder gently but firmly. "No. We must ride tomorrow, but you shall stay." He leaned over and whispered in Conachar's ear. "I will leave you in charge of Airchartdan. Hold it for me and the fortress will be yours when I return from Scone with the crown of Scotland on my head!"

CHAPTER SEVEN "THE JACOBITES"

They heard them coming from a mile away or more. Bagpipes skirling, drums beating, horses' hooves pounding on the hard pan road. The Ceardannan were gathered around the campfire for supper, consuming leftover venison stew and hard bread baked in Deidre's travelling oven, drinking sour berry wine brewed from their summer gatherings. Annie sat beside her brothers in the twilight watching George Urquhart across the flames, haggling over the price they would ask for the building materials in Drumnadrochit the next day. When the sound of the army approaching drowned out their conversation, all eyes shifted to the road. Geoffrey and her father remained seated without a word and watched them pass.

The Jacobites were an impressive bunch even if they hadn't the look of a uniformed army. Proudly marching in a variety of Clan kilts, rabbit-fur sporrans hanging from their belts, broad swords over their shoulders and knives tucked into their garters, their only conformity were the white cockades they wore on their Highland bonnets to show their loyalty to Bonnie Prince Charlie. Annie took them in with her young eyes, attracted to the stature of the younger men, some barely older than she was herself. Handsome young lads who had probably never left their family farms let alone fought in any wars. Yet, here they were, marching off to battle like truly seasoned soldiers. She was impressed and slightly smitten as any young girl would be. Beside her she could feel the tensing of Alex' shoulder against hers as the parade of men shuttled by. When she turned to look at him, she glimpsed a tear rolling down his cheek an instant before he could wipe it away.

"Alex? What's the matter with ya?"

The others around them remained sitting, their eyes downcast, silent.

"They are g'wine to fight for Prince Charlie," he whispered. "I wish I had their courage."

Annie looked again at the soldiers marching by. *Young boys going off to die*, she thought sadly. "Most of them willna' come home, Alex. They got their arses licked at Sherffmuir. They'll never be able to beat the English."

Alex' eyes changed suddenly from weeping softness to a hard stare. "You mustna' say that, Annie! Dinnae' curse them! They are fighting for our country. For Scotland's independence and our rightful king on the throne!"

She did not understand his emotion. "What does it matter who sits on the throne in England? Why must they *die* for it?"

For the first time in her life, she could see anger in her brother's face. Anger aimed at *her*! Suddenly he stood up and placed his hand over his heart as if saluting the passing army. Geoffrey and the others took notice of it too. Her father shook his head and whispered something to the leader of the Ceardannan. They both stared at Alex as did the others sitting around the fire. By the time the procession had passed, there was a low mumbling, and the gypsies were getting up to leave the circle, retiring to their tents and wagons. A few shot hostile glances toward Alex. She watched as Geoffrey and her father stood up and approached them. George was speaking into their leader's ear in desperate whispers. Annie could tell there was something terribly wrong.

"Boy, ye have made yer allegiance known," said Geoffrey. "We cannae' have no Jacobites in our group. The Ceardannan must remain neutral in these wars, or we'll be fighting amongst ourselves in no time. You had better pack your things and be off with ya!"

Annie couldn't believe her ears. She looked to her father to stop the insanity. Surely, he wouldn't allow Geoffrey to throw Alex out and abandon him! "Da! Alex is no Jacobite! Tell him!"

Alex turned toward her with a sad smile on his face. "I'm sorry, Annie, but I am. I have always been. The crown was stolen from us. I have always believed in the Stuarts' right to the throne."

"But Alex! You cannae' join their army! You could be killed!"

"That's what happens to soldiers on a fool's mission," said George, with a disappointed shrug. "They are chasing a hopeless dream."

Alex reached down and picked up his knapsack. He leaned in and whispered to Annie one last time. "I'll be back for ya, Annie. Dinnae' worry. You'll be safe with Angus and Da and Deidre. They'll watch over you."

There were tears in his eyes again, but Annie could tell they were a different kind of tears. They were not tears of anger; they were tears of *pride*.

He planted a hasty kiss on her cheek and shook his brother's hand before he turned and ran off down the road behind the army. George Urquhart walked away, and no final words were exchanged between father and son. Annie stood there for a few moments in disbelief, hoping to see Alex turn around and come back. The music from the pipes began to fade beneath the trees and the beating of the drums softened, muffled by the wind, and she realized her brother would never return. Gone off with the army to fight. Gone off with the army to die! Annie suddenly stood up and ran across the camp to her bed sack and retrieved her mother's tartan, squeezing the fabric in her hands as if to wring out all the tears she had shed into it over the years. She ran down the road after Alex and caught up with him at the edge of the woods.

"Here," she said, thrusting the ragged tartan into his hands. "Ye cannae' march into battle without the family colors."

Alex smiled down at her and drew her up into his arms, then released her reluctantly. He tucked her precious tartan beneath his belt. "Annie, please forgive me. I'll be back for ya, I promise! This is just something I have to do."

"I know," she said. "I dinnae' understand it but I know."

She turned and ran then, back toward the camp, down the hill to the bridge, to find a secluded spot on the bank to cry in solitude.

The sun had left and the water gurgling under the bridge had turned black. The toads were out, crooning to the stars. Her stomach was tied in knots, and she thought she might vomit, but strangely, her eyes remained dry. She could feel anger bubbling in her, anger toward Alex. How could he leave her now? He was all she had in the world! The only one who loved her. Annie felt abandoned and alone. She sat there well into the night, feeling dead on the inside, trying to make sense of what had happened. Part of her wanted to run after Alex. She wanted to plead and beg and scratch at his face with her fingernails if necessary. Her mother had left her years before but not by choice. Alex was leaving of his own free will, sacrificing his family for a faraway prince he had never met before. She closed her eyes and tried to blot out the darkness she felt seeping into her soul.

For hours she sat with her back against the stone pillar that held up the bridge, digging its rough knuckles into her spine.

As the evening mist began to drift in off the water and settle around her, she felt it begin to drip down her shoulders seeping beneath her bodice, mingling with her own tears that had finally begun to fall. *The castle is weeping with me*, she thought, for she had become part of the castle, and it a part of her. She wiped the tears and dew away from her face and stood up to leave when suddenly she felt a strange rush between her legs and a dampness creeping down her thighs from her private parts. Her abdomen curled inward, tightening like an angry fist, and she moaned from the sudden, unexpected pain. The neighbor women back in Cromarty had warned her this would happen one day. Strange that she had passed from girlhood to womanhood so suddenly and she felt no emotion, only lingering sadness at Alex' departure.

She limped up the steep incline toward the camp, clutching her gut. As she passed under the ring of night lanterns that stretched between the wagons, she looked down and noticed the large dark stain that had spread down her skirt, a sign she had become a woman but to Annie it held a much different meaning. Blood had begun to flow, from her, from the Jacobites, from Alex. She was sure it was a sign of what was to come.

Annie was awake and up before the sun the next morning in time to change her women's rags and clean herself. The cramps in her abdomen had weakened to a dull throbbing; the ache in her chest, while not physically manifested, was more acute, reminding her that her heart remained broken. The place at her feet where Alex had always been when she opened her eyes in the morning, watching over her, guarding her from harm, was now vacant. Nothing but trampled grass lay around her. Angus was a few yards away, just awakening from his sleep, rubbing his eyes and running his hand through his unruly hair. Her father had slept elsewhere, somewhere near Geoffrey's tent, no doubt.

"So that is the way of it then?" she said sourly. "We are just g'wine to leave our brother behind?"

Angus looked at her and shrugged. "It was his choice, Annie. If he wants to die for the cause, it is his own doing. Myself, I want to stay alive a little longer."

"You are just like Da! You are only interested in making a few schillings and getting drunk! You dinnae' care that Alex has gone off to die! I am ashamed of *both* of you!"

It wasn't what she had intended to say. With painful clarity she realized she had only Angus and her father left in the world. Perhaps she should be kind to them. Even if they did not care much about her, they were still the only family she had ever known, the last scraping from the bottom of the pot. With sad indifference, she rolled up her bedding and headed across the camp thinking only of returning to the tower to seek out the mysterious old woman. Some of the men, including her father, had hitched up several wagons to transport the spoils of the castle up the hill to the town of Drumnadrochit, with high hopes of finding gainful employment there. She heard George instruct Angus to stay behind and continue the demolition of the castle.

"You stay here with Angus," her Da told her firmly, "and, dinnae' get in your brother's way while we're gone."

She shrugged and watched them ride off in their wagons and disappear up the muddy road. She stopped to pet Bobbin where he was grazing on the bank and waved to Olin before she ran across the cobbled bridge and into the courtyard. She had to rid her mind of Alex who had deserted her. The castle and the search for the old woman would occupy her mind today. There were other men who stayed behind with Angus, and she saw them spread out across the bailey, her brother heading for the path that led down to the beach. He turned and waved goodbye to her, hoisting his gunny sack high over his shoulder. "Alex said there were good stones on the beach. I'm going to collect as many as I can find."

Annie thought about the strange stones someone had so meticulously stacked next to the water. She wanted to stay angry at him, but her emotions went suddenly flat. "Be careful," she said dully. "The Druids might be angry if'n you tear down their cairns."

Angus laughed and Annie smiled. She couldn't remember ever hearing him laugh out loud. He was always so sullen and quiet and although he had never been actually cruel to her, he had never spoken very kindly to her either. Now, she was acutely aware that he was the only brother she had left. She watched him walk toward the shore and turned her attention back to the tower above her. She ran toward the open door to put losing Alex out of her mind, forgetting everything except the possibility of seeing the old woman again.

The men of the Ceardannan were already at work inside wreaking even more destruction on the tower. The sound of their hammers and axes on the hard stone echoed down the stairwell from the upper floors. To avoid getting in their way she reached for the torch on the wall and started down into the dungeon to peruse the bowels of the ruin again on the chance the old woman might reappear. This time she noticed that as she descended the steps, the walls around her changed. The structured, mortared stone soon gave way to the original rock that formed a natural catacomb beneath the castle. The walls were damp and visibly weeping down onto the steps. A rat crossed her path on the stair, its red eyes glowing in the light of the torch, and she started. Rats didn't really scare her. They'd had plenty in the years they lived in Cromarty. She remembered hearing tales that the gypsies roasted and ate them. She hoped not. Surely, the people she was getting to know were more civilized than that.

Holding the torch above her head she shined its light on the walls, noticing for the first time the strange etchings on them, unfamiliar symbols and pictures. They made her think of the gravestones in the old cemetery back in Cromarty. Whether Norse runes or Pictish art she could not understand but they told *someone's* stories. She ran her hands over them and tried to imagine what *she* would write on a wall to tell her *own* story. Once again, she felt the familiar tremor in the very tips of her fingers. They spoke louder to her than the drawings on the walls but what the old castle was trying to tell her she did not know.

She shined the light into the crevices and recesses of the cave-like room, finding only bits of tangled fish nets and hooks, dried aquatic plants, and rodent skeletons among the rotted crates and casks, rat-hair nests and empty liquor bottles. In one corner, she found evidence of a recent fire, blackened wood and still-soft ash. Beside it she could see where the dust had been displaced, where someone had sat to warm themselves by the fire. *Was it her old woman*? she wondered. She sat down on the spot and looked around her, trying to imagine who the woman was and why she was here in the castle. Was she a Druid? A witch? Annie's mind was full of wonder and awe. After a few minutes, she decided to wait. Up from the locked grate she could hear the water ebbing and flowing below, gurgling around the rocks in the underground cave. It was a soothing sound; she drowsed to the lull of the water and soon fell asleep.

She awoke to the sound of loud footsteps clambering down the stairs. Someone was coming toward her in a hurry. She stood up quickly and watched the glow of a torch on the walls of the stairwell. When a face finally appeared in the darkness, she recognized her father instantly.

"Bloody hell, Annie, what are you doin' down here all alone?"

She was surprised he had even come looking for her. Her father had never expressed any concern over her welfare before.

"I was exploring," she replied, stretching sleepily. "I must have drifted off."

"Well, I've been lookin' all over for ya. I cannae' find Angus either. Come now and get up outta here then and help me find him. This is no place for a lass down here among the rats."

"I didn't think you cared," Annie mumbled under her breath, not loud enough for her father to hear. The only one who had ever cared about her was gone, off to fight with Prince Charlie.

Begrudgingly, she stood up and brushed herself off, following him back up the stairs and out into the courtyard to search for Angus. It was late afternoon already and the sun was hanging low over the hills. "He went down to the beach to gather stones, Da. I watched him go."

Out of curiosity, she followed along behind him, to the edge of the cliff; when they looked down, they saw Angus' gunny sack lying on the sand, half filled with stones. Angus was nowhere to be seen.

The slick mud on the incline had not dried much and the many footsteps going up and down had now hollowed out a crude path. They hurried down the bank.

"Angus?" George called out, looking up and down the beach. "Angus! Where are ya?"

Annie went north and her father went south up and down the shoreline, calling his name. With no luck, they turned around and headed back toward each other, meeting in the middle near Angus' abandoned sack.

"Maybe he went after Alex," she said coldly. "Maybe now you have lost *both* your sons."

It was then that Annie looked down at her feet. There, amidst the pebbles and shells she saw something very strange although she recognized them the instant she saw them. *Buttons!* Four tiny square wooden buttons, with two small holes in the center of each and fragments of thread still hanging off them. She reached down and picked them up, holding them in her upturned palm.

"What have you got there?" George asked, hoping it was something of value that could be sold or redeemed.

Something made Annie look upward at the windows in the tower, at eyes she just knew were staring back at her. She felt a cold chill deep in her core and her body convulsed.

"What is it? What's wrong with you?"

She held her hand out. "These were the buttons off Angus' shirt. I remember them because I sewed them on the day we left Cromarty."

George Urquhart growled and shook his head. "Damned fool!" he muttered and stomped back up the hill in anger.

When she had returned to the camp and joined the others around the supper fire, she listened to her father try to explain Angus' sudden disappearance to Geoffrey. George Urquhart did not seem at all concerned that he had lost another son. His only worry seemed to be his status in the Ceardannan. With two strong boys at his side, he could bargain a fair wage. Now his status had diminished. "He always was the lazy one. He's probably just gone back to Cromarty or off with his fool brother to fight for the Catholics! They'll come back with their tails 'tween their legs."

Annie had never been fond of Angus. His sullen demeanor did not elicit love and affection. Still, she was perplexed that her brother would just up and run off without a word. "It's not like him, Da. He never said anything to me aboot being unhappy here."

"And Alex couldna' keep his Jacobite sympathies to himself! Now, look at what I'm left with! My sons have abandoned me, and I am left with a useless girl who cannae' hold her tongue! Well, we dinnae' have time to go a'lookin' fer him. We've got work to do. Jobs a'waitin' in Drumnadrochit. Angus is a grown man and he kin make his own way. If that is what he chooses."

Annie took her supper and went off to her bed, knowing her sleep would be fitful that night, surprising even herself over her concern about Angus.

"Are ye worried aboot your brothers?"

It was Deidre, leaning over her shoulder, speaking in a low whisper.

"He might at least have said goodbye to us," Annie replied sadly. "I was not close to Angus like I was to Alex. But a goodbye would have been nice."

"Try not to worry," said Deidre. "Young men have to make their own way. You'll see them again, I'm sure. Meantime, you come to me for anything. I know your Da isn't the best of fathers. I kin see that. But you have a friend in me."

"Thank you, Deidre. That means a lot to me."

Looking down, the woman noticed the dark stain on the girl's skirt. Although Annie had scrubbed it vigorously on the rocks, it would probably be permanent. She only had one other dress that had grown too small for her, so it had to do for the time being.

"I have an old dress that might fit you," said Deidre. "I've grown too fat to wear it. Come to the wagon and I'll dig it out."

"But you will need it again after the bairn comes," Annie protested.

"Right now, you need it more than I do."

When morning came again, the men were up, making plans for the day's work. Annie made her way to Olin's spot after she had rolled up her bed and tucked it carefully away under Deidre's wagon. Bobbin was grazing nearby on the bank of the moat; Olin was warming himself in the morning sun, sorting through a pile of straw before he began his day's work.

"Your brother willna' be comin' back, Lassie."

"Do you mean Angus or Alex?"

Olin nodded with a sad smile. "Neither, I fear."

His words were short and prophetic. Annie sank down beside him on the bank. "Angus was never very happy working with Da and Alex has always been a closet papist, I am sure. He took after my Mum."

"Angus didna' leave of his own accord. I warned ya aboot the kelpie, didna? You best be watching yerself down there on the beach. Wild creatures always come back to their old feeding ground."

Annie shook her head, unwilling to believe such nonsense. Still, she couldn't help but think about the buttons. She fingered them in her pocket and decided to keep her mouth shut and not reveal that detail to Olin. "Angus has just gone out on his own, that is all. He's following Alex now or he's gone back home to Cromarty."

Olin laughed. "Believe what you wish," he said. "But dinnae' say I didna' warn ya!"

Today the old man was annoying her with his foreboding. It was a load too heavy for her to carry just now. She didn't want to argue with him. Alex leaving had been a shock. He never would have left her behind if he would have known that Angus would run off too. Now all she had was Da and to him she was invisible, a worthless girl. She had to extricate herself from the conversation to keep from bursting into tears. She hoisted up Deidre's skirt and patted the old man's shoulder.

"Good day to you, Olin."

CHAPTER EIGHT "THE HEALER"

Conachar's leg took many weeks to mend. The day after Malcom and his army had left Airchartdan, it had started to fester and swell. The cook and the housekeeper of the fortress tried everything they could think of, draining it with leeches, dousing it with ale and scrubbing it out with salt. Nothing seemed to help. At long last, they sent a messenger on horseback deep into the Great Glen to fetch a healing woman to come and exercise her magical powers on the dying man.

She came in the late afternoon, riding on the back of the messenger's horse. She was young and pretty but dressed all in white she looked pale and older than her years, and she carried a burlap bag over her shoulder. In it were her potions. But as pretty as she was, the messenger was glad to be rid of her. The bag reeked like rotten flesh and was attracting a horde of flies to its stench. She immediately jumped down from the horse and pushed her way into the great room in haste.

"Where is your injured man?" she asked the women inside. "Show me to him. I havna' got all day."

The cook led her up the stairs to the bedchamber where Conachar was laying in his bed. His eyes had grown over with the veil of a dying man. His skin had turned pallor. When he saw the woman, his lips upturned into a half-smile. He tried to extend his hand to her, but he could not; it fell weakly to his side.

The woman flung back the blanket on the bed and pulled up his nightshirt to inspect his wound. By that time, it had turned an angry red and was oozing yellow pus, the swelling visibly pulsing as if his body was trying to exorcise a demon. "Hold still," was all she said. With both hands she gripped his leg tightly and began to squeeze. Conachar screamed out in pain. "Stop, Woman! Are you trying to kill me?"

"Bring me towels and soap and water," was her command to the cook, who ran from the room more to escape from the cloud of stench that had filled the air.

"Who are you?" asked Conachar. "A gypsy?"

"Some say so," said the woman, never letting go of the putrid wound. "I have healed many wounds such as yours. It was the boar who did this, no?"

Conachar nodded weakly. "He killed my dog. I suppose I am the lucky one."

When the cook returned with the towels and soap, the woman mopped up the stinking puddle from the bed and poured water directly into the gaping wound on his leg. She began to scrub, swirling the soap around in brown bubbles while Conachar grimaced from the pain. "Bloody hell, Woman! I would not treat my horse so roughly!"

She shook her head. "Do you think a sword wound on the battlefield would hurt less? Be still, I say. I am trying to work here."

She was gruff and her bedside manner was not unlike that of the boar who had inflicted the wound, but she seemed to know what she was doing, however painful it was to Conachar. After an hour of torture, the patient had collapsed into a deep sleep.

"Where are his breeches?" she asked the cook.

The woman pointed to a pile of clothing in the corner of the room and watched as she took and knife and cut a large bloody piece from the pant leg where the boar had ripped them apart. She deposited the cloth into her smelly bag and walked briskly out of the room, searching for the man on whose horse she had arrived. "I'll return tomorrow and the next day until he is well," she told the cook. "He'll live."

The following morning, once again, they sent the rider into the woods to shuttle her back to Conachar's bedside and she repeated the rough treatment of the first day. The swelling had gone down, and the boil had faded from an angry red to a docile pink.

"How are you today?" she asked as she inflicted more pain on him.

"A little better, I think," replied Conachar. "I must admit I thought you were going to be the death of me yesterday, but you clearly know what you are doing. I thank you."

"You will get stronger with each day if you rest and follow my orders. Death will not find you while you are under this roof."

It was an odd thing to say and Conachar wondered about it afterwards. What did she mean "while he was under this roof"? Did she know something he did not? Did she somehow know that he would have been slain on the battlefield had he gone off to fight with Malcom? Was it an omen that he should live if he stayed within the walls of Airchartdan? Was the woman a seer as well as a healer? After she had gone, the cook brought him his supper and for the first time since his encounter with the boar he felt hunger and thirst return to his gut. It was then Conachar knew he was on the mend.

Within another week, he was up and walking, surveying the courtyard. While he was waiting, he decided he might as well make improvements to the fortress, to prepare for Malcom's triumphant homecoming. He assigned his men to cut wood and replace the rotting planks in the fortress walls and gather stones for the building of a palisade all around it. Every day he grew stronger and more determined. If Malcom returned, this place would belong to him, and he was determined to make it the most formidable fortress in Scotland. He drew plans for outbuildings, stables, dovecots and a proper chapel. He hired more men from the small town on the hill and soon the entire courtyard was buzzing with sawblades and the pounding of hammers on stone.

The healer only came once a week, now that she knew her patient was mending nicely. Conachar wanted to repay her in some way for saving his life but what could she possibly want? She lived in obscurity deep in the woods where she performed her rituals and survived on the meager gleanings of the earth. Gold and silver meant nothing to her. When she visited him the next time, he greeted her at the gate and invited her in to show her the progress he was making on the improvements. The expression in her eyes told him she was pleased.

"You have breathed new life into the stones," she said, nodding and smiling, showing slightly crooked teeth. "Emchath would reach up from his grave and give you thanks if he could."

"My ancestor built this place," he said. "It will be mine when Malcom returns."

"Malcom has nothing to do with it. This would be your home regardless of who sits on the throne of Scotland. The name of your family is embedded in the stone."

He liked the sound of that, of his God-given right to the fortress even though he knew that Malcom would have a stronger claim were he to become king. The healer was right;

his family had built this place from nothing and had held it for years. That had to mean *something*.

"By the way," he said. "I do have one complaint. It is aboot that perfectly good pair of riding breeches that I wore the day the boar attacked me. They could have been washed and mended. Why did you see fit to cut them into pieces?"

She cocked her head and shrugged. "Why I took the cloth to the Clootie Well, of course."

"The *what*?"

"Ye have never heard of the Clootie Well? They dinnae' have them in Ireland?"

Conachar remembered an old faerie tale from his childhood. Something about a magical spring in the woods that could heal wounds. He never believed it.

"Is that what healed me? Are you really just a pretender? And here I thought you could actually speak to the gods."

"Aye," said she, "that is what I am. I pretend to be a conduit to the faeries."

"Well, I have been racking my brain as to how I can repay you for your service. Perhaps I should offer up a bloody sacrifice in your name instead."

"You should pay homage to the ground on which you stand."

Conachar laughed. "Well, what can I give you? Surely, there must be something! What do I have in my possession that would please you?"

The woman thought for a long moment. She turned and looked back at Conachar. "I could use a warm bed come winter."

"That you shall have! Any room you choose!"

"I think I prefer the catacomb *beneath* the fortress," she said. "It suits me."

CHAPTER NINE "ABANDONED"

"Annie, you must come back to the camp!"

It was Deidre hurrying down the rocky shore toward her, flailing her arms in the air. Annie was returning from her walk along the water's edge. She raised her hand to shade her eyes from the glaring sun. "Why? What has happened?"

"It's your Da! He's in a bad way! You must come, Annie! Please!"

She had seen her father earlier that day, heading off across the bridge with the other men with a pickaxe slung over his shoulder. The men of the Ceardannan had made a handsome profit the previous day, selling off the stones and lumber they had scavenged from the castle, and they were determined to plunder even more. Annie looked into Deidre's eyes and could see the worry in them. "But what has happened?"

Deidre reached out and clutched the girl's hand firmly. "They were trying to bring down those standing stones in the courtyard. An unbroken stone of that size would bring a handsome price from the stone masons in Drumnadrochit."

"Did the stone fall on him?"

Deidre didn't answer right away. She was struggling to climb the steep incline and keep Annie's hand in hers when she suddenly clutched her stomach and let out a moan. When she finally reached the top, she turned and dropped her hand.

"What is it, Deidre? Is it the bairn?"

Deidre sank to the earth. "I will be alright. I just need to stop and rest for a moment." She paused to catch her breath. "I know you and your Da dinnae' see eye to eye on things, Annie, but he is still your Da. He has been hurt and it is your place to care for him. He asked for you."

Annie doubted that. Her father was always telling her to go away, to not get underfoot, to be invisible and silent as she performed her chores. Now, he *needed* her? She scoffed at the suggestion. "Did the rock fall on his *head*? Is that what this is all aboot?"

Deidre shook her head. "No, it's worse than that I am afraid. It was just a tiny piece of rock. Hardly made a mark but now...."

"But now *what*?"

"You'll see. But you must come. He needs you now."

Annie helped Deidre to her feet. "Are you sure you are alright?"

Deidre nodded. They walked across the bridge, but Annie refused to hurry. Her father had never gone out of his way to pay attention to her except to criticize. Never a word of praise. Never a compliment over a well-cooked meal or a clean house. She followed Deidre into the camp and saw her father lying on his bed sack near their wagon. His leg was elevated on a crate and his pant leg had been rolled up, exposing his hairy shin.

"You asked for me, Da?" There was the slightest hint of sarcasm in her voice. There was no reply. She hoped he was now realizing his daughter was all he had left and that, maybe, he would begin to treat her with respect.

He turned his head toward her, but his eyes did not seem to focus. It was as if he was in a daze. *Why, he's just drunk*! she thought miserably. Annie looked down at his leg and saw a tiny red wound. All this fuss for a scratch? Then she noticed a strange blue line that ran from the wound up his leg, disappearing beneath the knee of his breeches. She turned to

Deidre who was standing nearby. "Are you sure it isna' a snake bite?"

At that moment, Geoffrey came forward. "No, a piece of the rock broke and a flying chip pierced his leg. It must be some type of poison. He's gone delirious and he's talking like a mad man, not making any sense at all."

"Perhaps he shouldna' been drinking whiskey before he started breaking up rocks."

At her impertinence, Geoffrey puffed out his chest and glared at her. "He had no whiskey. None of us were drinking. We had work to do and your Da was just doing his job. How disrespectful you are, Lass! You should mind your tongue!"

The leader of the Ceardannan spun on his heal and walked away. Deidre put her hand on Annie's shoulder. "He's right, Annie. He *is* your Da after all and he is the only family you have left."

Annie turned again to her father. "Da, look at me. Have you been drinking? Have you a secret flask in your pocket that Geoffrey doesna' know aboot?"

George Urquhart blinked and then closed his eyes.

"No, Annie," said Deidre. "He had no whiskey. My husband tells the truth. There must have been an evil man buried beneath that stone. See how the poison is spreading up his leg?"

Annie knelt beside her father and inspected the wound and the strange blue streak. "I've never heard of a poison stone before."

"No, nor have I," said Deidre sadly shaking her head, "but I am beginning to think this castle is cursed. You've lost your brothers and now this."

"Alex went off to join the Jacobites. That can hardly be blamed on the castle."

"But your other brother? Disappearing like that. There is something strange aboot this place, and it gives me an uneasy feeling."

Suddenly Annie thought about the strange old woman she had seen in the stairwell. She remembered the buttons and the feeling that eyes were following her from the windows of the tower. She looked into Deidre's eyes.

"Maybe it is the Druids," said a voice behind them.

This time it was Olin who came forward. Annie snapped out of her trance. She looked at the old man and smiled. "I think not, Olin. My Da has a secret bottle of whiskey around somewhere. 'Twasn't the Druids or the rock or the kelpie that did this. It was whiskey sure."

"I warned you that the Druids were not anyone to trifle with. They have serious black magic."

"Olin, I dinnae' believe in black magic. That is silly. My Da will be better in the morning when he has slept it off."

She retrieved her bed sack from the grassy bank and spread it out near her father, more to please the others and save face in front of those who thought she was a disrespectful child with no compassion. No one understood how a daughter could be so insensitive to her father's condition. He was sleeping now, snoring as was his way. It was a warm night but the breeze off the water was brisk and cool, and she dutifully covered him with the blanket Angus had left behind. Deidre did not ask her for help with the supper dishes. She brought Annie a bowl of porridge and a hunk of bread, instead.

"I'll just be here in the wagon if you need me," she said. "Try to be kind to him, Annie."

There were no stars that night for the clouds had settled in over the loch. As Annie stretched out, she yearned to rest her head on her mother's tartan, but she was glad she had given it to Alex. He needed it more than she. She realized now she could be banished from the Ceardannan for displaying their clan tartan, remembering sourly how they had run poor Alex away for simply showing support for the Jacobites. She stared upward into the night but all she could see above her was a blanket of grey fog that encircled the flames of the camp torches like rings of soft fur. Geoffrey and the other men were still sitting by the fire, but their mood seemed more subdued than usual. Several of them glanced back toward Annie and her father and they appeared to be lowering their voices so she could not hear what they were saying. She heard the word "cursed" in the whispers. She had the uneasy feeling they were talking about her family. She closed her eyes and tried to make herself fall asleep, but sleep would not come to her. Deidre was right about one thing; Da was the only family she had left. Alex might be dead by now and who could say where Angus was.

Listening to his snoring beside her, she suppressed the urge to reach out and pinch him, to disturb his sleep, to punish him for dragging their family away from Cromarty on this foolish quest. What had it gained them? It was just the two of them now, a girl and her drunken father. Would she now be condemned to nursing a man who had never had any use for her except to put supper on the table and sweep the floor? Was she now expected to feel compassion and sympathy for him when all her life he had barely spoken a kind word to her?

How could she had lived under the same roof with him all her life and only now be realizing how much she truly hated him? She couldn't blame her brothers for running away. He was no more affectionate to them than he was to her. But did they have to abandon her too? How she missed having a mother at that moment!

She laid there silently until the entire camp had gone to sleep in their wagons and tents and a stillness set in before she gathered up her bedclothes and tiptoed out of the camp, treading softly on the grass until she reached the bridge. She had intended to sleep on the bank of the river, but tonight something pushed her on and she crossed over. The cobbles were cold against her bare feet sending shivers up her legs. She ran under the portcullis and across the courtyard to the tower door. Every day after her chores were finished, she had returned to the dungeon beneath the castle to search for the mysterious old woman. Tonight, she would try searching in the darkness.

Inside, the torches were dying in their sconces. When she reached up and grabbed the one at the top of the stair to light her way, it sputtered and went out completely and she found herself surrounded by total blackness. The stairwell to the dungeon was like a dark funnel and she inched along, guiding herself by the curve of the walls. She knew the way so well now; she had visited the dungeon many times. Down, down, down. Into the bowels of the castle ruins, descending into the arms of stone that cradled her, finding her way to her favorite corner, out of sight, where she spread out her bed hastily and flung herself down on it, resting her back against the rock wall. Frustration and hopelessness surrounded her like the darkness. She did not want to return to the camp. She did not want to be a nurse to her father who had never loved her. For the first time in her life, she wanted to close her eyes and *die.*

But she did *not* die. She had laid awake most of the night, uncomfortable on her bed of stone and cold beneath her blanket for the air beneath the castle was taking on the crisp fall air outside with no afternoon sun to warm it. She had finally fallen into a fitful sleep and when she opened her eyes, she knew she had overslept; she would not be able to slip back into camp unnoticed. She would have to ignore the disappointment in Deidre's eyes and the scowl on Geoffrey's face. Most of all she had to go back to nursing her Da from his hangover. "Well, I hope he's done puking at least," she thought miserably, "so I dinnae' have to clean *that* up."

She sat up and rolled up her bedding in the darkness and started for the stairwell, inching along the wall, moving her feet slowly along the uneven stone floor. When she reached the first step, she guided herself with one hand while clutching her blanket in the other until she got to the top and the light from the courtyard made her blink until her eyes adjusted.

There were no men in the courtyard this morning, no sound of pounding hammers and chisels, no masculine voices echoing within the stone walls. Maybe they had all decided to get drunk like her father the night before and pass the jug around the campfire. Maybe they were *all* hungover this morning. But, no, they had all been asleep in their wagons and tents when she had tiptoed out of the camp. She was sure of it.

The morning sun was bright but not enough to take away the chill in the air and she shivered slightly and wrapped her blanket around her shoulders as she passed through the gatehouse. All at once, she froze, staring across the bridge at the banks on the other side, at the field and the road beyond. *The Ceardannan were gone!* The camp, the wagons, the tents, everything was gone! She began to run, slowly at first, then her feet broke into a frantic pace; her eyes filled with tears. How could they have abandoned her too? That her father had

94

deserted her did not surprise her but her brothers, Deidre, Olin? How could they all have left her there to fend for herself?

Her eyes searched the field beyond the riverbank, now a beaten, empty circle of trampled grass, a cold ashy pit where the campfire had been, and deep ruts where the wagons had pulled out. They had left nothing, no signs of any kind behind that they had even been there. She stopped running when she realized there was nothing to run after, no one to call out to. Even her father. They had all left her. Looking up and down the road she saw nothing and no one in either direction. She stopped near the spot where she had left him and his wounded leg, where she had reluctantly tucked him under Angus's blanket. The final abandonment, the last act of treachery. Annie sank to her knees and began to sob loudly. She hoped the gypsies up the road could hear her wail. She *wanted* them to hear her. It was at that moment it dawned on Annie. They thought the family was cursed! They must have thought she had disappeared too, just like Angus. Stupid, superstitious gypsies, always looking for sinister signs and omens.

Then, looking out between eyelashes that were heavy with tears, she saw it. The final blow. There on the bank was a patch of disturbed soil where the grass had once been. In the middle of the bare spot was a small crude cross sticking crookedly out of the ground. She jumped up and ran to it. On the crossbeam, gouged in the green bark, someone had carved a name.

George Urquhart.

CHAPTER TEN "WAITING"

Conachar and his men continued to make improvements to the fortress over the weeks and months that followed. There had been no word from Malcom, no news of any battles won or lost. The weather was changing now, and they were storing up firewood for the winter. Nighttime now brought freezing temperatures to the shores of Loch Ness; in the mornings the sand and stone were laced with frost, and icicles dripped from the overhanging eaves. Soon the roads would be snowed under and impossible for an army to pass. Conachar began to worry that he would be trapped in the fortress until the spring, but he had promised to hold and defend it for Malcom, and he was determined to keep his word.

The healer had moved her possessions from the woods into the dark recesses below the building; from time-to-time strange odors drifted up the stairwell and into the living quarters of Conachar's men. At night she could be heard reciting rituals and incantations in her Gaelic tongue. The men were afraid of her, of her spells and witchcraft, and they begged Conachar to send her back to the forest from whence she had come. But their leader was not afraid of the woman. He reminded his men that she had saved his life from the boar attack. He would not send her out in the wintertime to freeze to death.

So, no one except Conachar ever ventured down the spiral staircase into the catacomb she now called home and for months nothing bad or evil happened to the soldiers who lived within the fortress walls. He would visit her once or twice every week, finding her sitting in a corner by a small fire with tokens of her magic all around her and they would talk for hours about Scotland, the Picts and the history of the land that was now his home. For someone so young, he was surprised at her vast knowledge. She seemed to have lived through all the important events he had only heard stories about.

"Just how old *are* you?" he asked one day after she had finished telling him tales of the great King Duncan, of how his sons, Malcom III and Donald Bane, had fled with their mother to England as children to escape murder at the hands of Macbeth.

The woman smiled and tilted her head into a sidelong glance. "I have seen many summers," was her reply, "and many winters. I'm afraid I have lost count."

"But you look so young. You do not look a day over twenty! How could you have seen all these things in your lifetime? Surely, you have been told these tales by a bard or heard the words sung in a song!"

"I dinnae listen to faerie tales," she replied. "I listen to the stones. They speak the truth."

"Stones cannae' talk," said Conachar.

She looked at him then, her eyes piercing and steady. "Here," she said, taking hold of his hand and placing it on the stone wall. "Just listen."

Conachar was taken aback. He wasn't sure which was colder, the stone or the healer's hand. For a moment he humored her, out of respect, out of curiosity. It was then he felt it, a slight tremor tickling his palm, sending ripples of gooseflesh up his forearm. He drew his hand back and rubbed it against his shirt. "What was that?"

She smiled. "Those were the stones speaking to you."

He tried to make sense of it, to find a rational explanation for the vibration in the wall. "Surely, it is just the water rushing

97

beneath the castle, the waves hitting the rocks on the shore. Nothing more."

Her strange talk was making him uncomfortable. Some things were better left unsaid, some questions better left unanswered. Her magic had saved him once and he believed she had powers beyond those of mortal men, but it frightened him a little. He didn't want to understand it. It was safer to let it remain a mystery.

"Aye," she said quietly. "Of course, you are right. It is just the water."

"Tell me more about Malcom. I want to know him. What can you tell me about this king I intend to serve?"

She rubbed her hands together to take away the chill from her fingers and stared into the fire. "What is it you wish to know?"

"Will he be successful in defeating Macbeth? Will he be crowned king soon?"

"You mustn't hate Macbeth. He has as much right to the throne of Scotland as Malcom does."

"How can you say that? He is but a usurper!"

Her eyes narrowed. "Truth be told he has a legitimate claim to the throne as does your hero Malcom. His mother was the daughter of Malcom II. It is true he slayed the king, but it was a fair fight between two rivals. It is just as fair that Malcom has returned from his exile to fight for the crown."

How could that be true? Conachar wondered. "But the stories...."

"Never mind the stories you hear," replied the healer. "Scotland has seen many kings and will see many more. Macbeth is not the worst. Your Malcom may not be the best."

Conachar recognized the words of a traitor to his cause. The woman had saved his life but now she was talking treason. His loyalty to Malcom was being tested. "Lady, you are speaking against my king. I will not listen to it any further."

He stood up and began to leave.

"I am not loyal nor disloyal to Malcom or Macbeth or any king," she said. "I follow a power beyond any mortal sitting on a throne."

"You saved my life. In return, I have been kind to you and allowed you to stay here in the fortress. I'll not have you disrespect Malcom in the presence of my men. You will keep your opinions to yourself."

"Agreed," she said with a shrug. "You asked me to tell you things and I obliged you. If I have offended you, Conachar, I apologize. I speak my mind and my tongue always tells the truth, as I see it."

She was a strange one, this healer from the woods, this woman with special powers. Conachar was a little afraid of her, of her supernatural gifts and talents. He couldn't help but wonder if she spoke the truth, if Macbeth and Malcom were equally matched, if both had a rightful claim to the throne of Scotland. For the first time since he had come to Airchartdan she had made him feel unsure of himself and doubtful of his allegiance to Malcom. Had he come all this way from Ireland on a fool's mission? He went on about the daily business of improving the fortress that day, acting as if nothing were amiss. He had to keep his spirits up for his men. He could not look weak, or unsure, or defeated. He needed to stay strong until the king's return!

CHAPTER ELEVEN "COBLAITH"

Annie refused to give up. While instinctively she wanted to follow the Ceardannan up the road and beg Deidre to take her along to help with the bairn and the cooking, the stubborn side of her was angry. Angry they would leave her behind like that. Like her brothers had. She felt a little guilty about her father, about leaving him when he was injured. But what could she have done? She was no healer. No, whatever killed her Da was of his own doing and she had nothing to do with it.

She approached the question of how she was going to survive all alone, logically and calmly. She could gather berries and roots in the woods. She had never trapped a hare or caught a fish but if others could do it why couldn't she? She was fourteen, now a grown woman by the menstrual clock, capable of surviving on her own and besides, if Alex ever came back to look for her, he would come here first. *If* he ever came back, that is. She sat on the bank near her father's grave for a few moments to think and make a plan. Above her the tower loomed. The morning sun bounced off it, warm golden rays against the grey mortared stone. That was where she would live, she decided. She would make a home for herself deep in the dungeon where no one would find her; she would gather wood for winter fires and the last of the summer rowan berries and pull up what vegetables were left of the discarded garden in the courtyard. She had to be careful with mushrooms and only pick the ones she knew to be safe. For a brief moment she thought of making her way up the hill to the little town of Drumnadrochit to see what she could steal. "There you have it, Annie Urquhart!" she said out loud. "You lived with the Ceardannan long enough to become a common thief!"

She spent the better part of the day collecting things she thought she would need, removing her apron and tying it into a makeshift gunny sack to hoist over her shoulder. Inside the half-collapsed gatehouse, she found an old wooden bucket that was grey and warped with age but would still hold water and she filled it from the river. The toads were there watching her, their bulbous brown eyes blinking lazily, their haunches ready to leap into the water at the slightest threat. "Watch out," she warned them. "I may become a frog-eater yet."

By the end of the day, she had collected every spent torch she could find and wrapped them with strips she had torn from the hem of Deidre's dress, for it dragged the ground anyway. She then scraped pitch from the trees and gathered moss and pinecones from the forest floor, anything that would fuel a flame. She dug up the last carrots and turnips from the garden, picked through every piece of bruised fruit from the fallen trees in the courtyard until she had a small cache of edible food. She knew she could not afford to waste anything, not with the long winter approaching. She took it all back to the catacomb where she made a cozy nest in the deepest recess. She had no straw, so she piled dried leaves and chunks of soft moss to serve as a mattress over which she spread her blanket. Annie did not know when darkness had fallen, being so deep in her stone abode, but finally her weariness told her it was time to rest. After eating a withered apple and a misshapen carrot, she washed them down with a handful of water from her bucket. Then she snuffed out the torch so as not to waste it and settled herself in for sleep.

Her dreams were vivid that night. She dreamed she had returned to Cromarty and was searching for her brothers along the sea wall. She could feel the waves crashing around her and she could see English ships approaching the harbor, their cannons booming and filling the air with smoke. She found herself running up the street, looking for someone she knew but no one was there. It was as if they had all abandoned the town, leaving it to the English. On the hill, the old castle still stood, taunting her, shutting her out. When she ran up the hill toward the familiar grey walls, she found the great gates open, but just as she reached it the iron portcullis was slammed down, nearly skewering her to the ground. Thrashing around in the dirt she shook herself awake.

"I have my *own* castle now," she said aloud as she sat up, trembling.

She looked around in the darkness, thinking she heard footsteps on the upper floors. *It is just the wind,* she told herself and she laid down again and closed her eyes. But then she heard it again. Sure enough, there was someone descending the stairs, a flickering light from a torch was bouncing off the walls, coming closer. She had no weapon to defend herself, so she retreated deeper into the corner, drawing her knees up to her chest and hugging them tightly. Had someone come to look for her? Had the guilt of leaving her behind overpowered Deidre's heart? Had Alex returned from the war? Suddenly she felt more alone than ever.

She watched as a figure emerged from the stairwell, a small silhouette, not bulky enough to be Deidre, not nearly tall enough to be her brother. Maybe Deidre had given birth to her bairn, and she had grown thin again. Annie strained her eyes to see who was behind the light. Would it be friend or foe?

And there *she* was again: the old woman she had been searching for, stepping out of the darkened stairwell. Her gait was slow and unsteady, like all old people, and as she came forward, she looked into the corner, directly into Annie's eyes, like an owl or a cat that could see in the night. Annie took a deep breath and started to speak but the old woman spoke first.

"So, they have gone off and left ya, have they?"

Her voice was brittle like the splitting of old wood. She leaned the torch she was holding against the wall and sat down near Annie's bed, studying the girl's campsite: the wood pile, the water bucket, the bed of leaves and moss, the dwindling fire.

"Ya shouldna' be burning the rowan wood," she said simply. "Sacred wood of the Druids. Only to be used in rituals and blessings."

Annie found her voice. "Are you a Druid?"

The old woman cackled like a hen over her morning egg. "I'm not sure what I am. I used to look for the good in people but there ain't much good in this world these days. I have more faith in the earth and sky and water."

"That's not a very promising attitude," said Annie.

"Oh, and *you* are one to talk to *me* about attitude, are ya? You who left your Da to die with the Ceardannan?"

Annie was shocked that the old woman knew so much about her personal life. Had she been spying on her all this time? "How do you know that?"

"This was my home and you all invaded it. I see what I see. I know that you all stole from me and from your descendants." She stopped and shook her head sadly. "*You* of all people."

"Why *me* of all people? What have *I* got to do with it? I had no choice in the matter. My Da joined the gypsies and brought us here."

"You Urquharts are a queer bunch, I'll give ya that." She reached over and cupped her hands and helped herself to a drink from the bucket. "So do you intend to stay here now?"

Annie shrugged. "I have nowhere else to go. My family is gone. The Ceardannan have deserted me."

"Ya know for a fact that your brothers are dead, do ya?"

"Well, no, not exactly. But Alex is fighting with the Jacobites and Angus, well, I dinnae' know where *he is.*"

"Then I guess you'll be wantin' to stay here with me. Mind you, I like my peace and quiet. No hysterics." She paused and locked glances with Annie. "You ain't the hysterical type, are ya?"

"No, I'm not," Annie replied indignantly. "I am quite mature for my age. I have lost my entire family, and do you see me crying aboot it?"

What a nerve this old woman had, talking to her like that! It irritated Annie but she almost wanted to laugh. She and Olin would make an evenly matched pair!

"I'm only letting you stay because of who you are, mind ya, but dinnae' get any ideas about lordin' over me. I'm too old for that. You mind yer business and I'll mind mine and we'll get along just fine."

The air was getting colder. Annie pulled her blanket up around her shoulders and stoked the fire. "Might I know your name at least?"

"Name's Coblaith."

"Well, I am pleased to make your acquaintance, Coblaith. I am………"

The old woman wrapped her ragged shawl around her and stretched out by the fire. "I know who *you* are, Lassie."

There was no more conversation. Annie quieted all the questions that were bouncing around in her head, saving them for another time. They both slept then, and Annie felt a strange comfort in not being alone. Even if the old woman was crotchety and rude, at least she was company, someone to talk to. She missed Deidre. Most of all she missed Alex. But she feared that neither of them was coming back. Ever.

When morning came, Annie awoke to find that the old woman had set the rowan wood aside, replacing it with wych elm branches and was stoking the fire with tinder and kindling she had collected before the dawn. She had stretched an iron rod between two stones and had hung an old pot which was gurgling and bubbling with a pungent witch's brew. It did not smell like any food she was familiar with. Annie wrinkled her nose.

"If'n you want fancy food, ye had better cook for yerself," said Coblaith.

Annie pulled out her knapsack and rifled through its contents. "I found these carrots and turnips in the courtyard," she offered.

The old woman watched as Annie broke the vegetables into smaller pieces and did not object as she dropped them into the pot.

While their breakfast simmered, Coblaith stood up, relighting her torch in the fire and walked across the floor to the locked grate. She dug into her pocket and pulled out a large, skeleton key.

"You have the key?" Annie marveled. "I've been wondering, what is down there? Is it the sewer from the castle?"

"It used to be a prison. Many years ago."

Coblaith unlocked the grate and opened it slowly, letting it fall back with a loud bang that echoed off the rock walls. Holding the torch above her head, she climbed down carefully into the hole. Annie watched as she disappeared into the blackness and jumped up to follow her.

Beneath the catacomb was another compartment unlike any Annie had ever seen. The walls were as black as obsidian; the flame from the torch danced across them like amber ghosts in flight. All around the perimeter, just above the water, was a wide ledge where Coblaith apparently kept her personal belongings, a collection of baskets and boxes, tools and pots, a haphazard mix of junk from outward appearances. Beneath the ledge the water pulsed up and down, from where she could not see. There was no light, no visible opening anywhere, but it had the distinct damp smell of the lake. What little air there was was stale and dead, and Annie felt as if she needed to gasp to keep from suffocating. The old woman turned and handed the torch to Annie to free up her hands. "Hold this."

Annie took the torch and held it up high to light their path. From out of the darkness, she could see the ceiling of the cave and when she did, she flinched and took a step backward, aghast at the sight of dozens of black creatures suspended from it, seemingly in midair. She had never seen bats before, but she had heard they were hideous things with bulging eyes and sharp teeth. They appeared to be sleeping now, their wings folded, their eyes and mouths closed, clinging to the walls and ceiling of the cave.

"Ye need not be afraid of them," said Coblaith. "They do us no harm. They have been living down here for hundreds of years. Long before you or I."

"How *ever* did they get in here? How do they get *out*? Bats cannot swim, can they?"

Coblaith smiled a strange smile. "They manage."

She was rummaging through the contents of what looked like a small sea chest as if searching for something in particular. Finally, she pulled up a small tin box. Annie watched as she reached inside and pulled out two coins. She found two faded blankets that she tucked under her arm, and a strange, forked piece of wood, before replacing the box inside the chest and closing the lid. "I found what I need," she said and motioned for Annie to lead the way back up through the grate. When they had crawled through, Coblaith tossed the blankets to Annie. "Here," she said gruffly. "Shake the cobwebs outta them. The nights are getting colder." She then replaced the rusty padlock and locked it with the key.

"What is that?" Annie was curious. The strange piece of wood had been obviously whittled and planed, its bark removed, and the white flesh underneath polished with care. It was no ordinary branch; it was a tool of some sort. Or a weapon. She wasn't sure which.

Coblaith's eyes shifted as if she was not sure she wanted to reveal a secret. She handed the two coins to Annie. "Can ye take these up the hill to town and get us a bag of oats and a bag of salt?"

"I-I have never been to town," Annie stuttered.

"First time for everything, then," replied Coblaith. "I have other chores to do. You will carry your weight around here or

107

you can move on. Didna' livin' with the Ceardannan teach you that, Lassie?"

"Aye."

"Then go! Before the morning is away, I have work to do!"

Annie reluctantly took the coins and two empty bags before she picked up the torch to guide herself up the stairs. At the top she snuffed it out, dropping it into the empty sconce on the wall, and walked out into the courtyard in the warm morning sunshine. It seemed strange for the place to be deserted now that she had become accustomed to the sounds of the gypsies working. She passed through the gatehouse and over the bridge, stopping to speak to the toads on the riverbank before she found her feet carrying her up the road toward Drumnadrochit. She knew it was only a mile or two at the most. The road was uneven and rocky, and she kept her eyes to the ground to keep from stumbling, forced to stop once to let a meandering flock of sheep cross over in front of her. The incline was gradual but before too long she knew she was travelling upward; the breeze off the water picked up her hair and scattered it about. When she stopped and turned back, she could see she was far above the old castle. The midday sun was dazzling on the granite stones and shimmering on the loch. Wiping the sweat from her brow she increased her pace, anxious to finish her shopping errand and return to familiar surroundings.

When she finally reached the crest of the hill, the town came into view. A cluster of rock dwellings with thatched roofs and smoke curling from the chimneys. The stream doubled back, and she had to cross over a bridge. She paused only long enough to look for toads on the banks below before she set foot on the narrow, cobbled street.

There was a church, the tallest structure in the little town, with stained glass windows and a bell tower, surrounded by a small graveyard with tall grass among the headstones, reminding her of her father's simple grave outside the gate of the castle. No stones for paupers. Was that what she was now? A pauper? For sure, an orphan, with no parents and brothers gone off to lands faraway. All she had now was……. Coblaith.

When she found the center of town, she knew it was the center because it was where the local tavern was situated. Her Da had always said that the tavern was the heart of any town. It was a dingy little place, much like the one her father had frequented back in Cromarty; its door was standing open and when she passed, the familiar stench of ale drifted out on the breeze. She wrinkled her nose repugnantly. She was sure her father had visited it with Geoffrey and the others during their stay. It brought back unhappy memories.

The next building was a tannery that reeked of dead animals and overpowered the smell of the tavern. She walked on, passing a small shop with housewares on display in a tiny grimy window that suggested a merchant. She retraced her steps and opened the door,

"Can I help you, Lassie?" asked a middle-aged portly woman who stood behind a wooden counter with her hands on her hips. "You want to buy somethin'?"

The woman's eyes were suspicious. Annie could feel it in her cold stare. Did she know she had once been associated with the Ceardannan? Did she think she had come to steal?

"I need some salt and oats, please." She placed her empty bags on the table.

The woman sighed. "Three half-pennies. Have you got that much? Dinnae' bother me if'n you havna'.'"

Annie opened her hand and showed the woman the coins. "I only have two, Mum. Can you give me just *this* much?"

Grunting for her inconvenience, the woman took the two bags and opened first one and then the other, filling them from bins behind her. She grabbed the two coins from Annie's palm before she set the bags down on the counter.

"Thank you, Mum," Annie said politely, with a shallow curtsey. She really wanted to stick her tongue out at the woman for being so rude, but she turned and exited the shop, bags in hand, eager to be away from the town and the smell of ale and dead animals. As she hurried down the main street, she met people passing but they stared at her too, frowning, not friendly as the people back in Cromarty had been. These were not her neighbors. These people saw her as an outsider, a foreigner. She did not belong here; their eyes were telling her: *Go away little orphan girl.*

Going downhill was much quicker than the trip up, and Annie had to pace herself to keep from slipping on the stones. When she reached the halfway mark where the sheep were quietly grazing on the side of the road, she stopped to catch her breath. Annie smiled at a pair of lambs frolicking in the tall grass. She missed Bobbin and Olin. Why had everyone and everything in her life gone away? There was a strange emptiness within her, almost like a hunger for food. She looked back up the hill toward the little town of Drumnadrochit and then back toward the castle below at the edge of the water. She belonged in neither place; she could call neither place her home.

By the time she reached the bridge, she ran across it eagerly, hoping to impress Coblaith with her promptness in completing her assigned task but when she reached the catacomb, the old woman was nowhere in sight and the grate was still locked. Annie left the bags of salt and oats in the corner and climbed the stairs again to search for her.

The grass across the courtyard was waving gently; the breeze off the water had become brisker and cooler. Autumn was setting in. Annie walked to the edge of the cliff that overlooked the shoreline and shaded her eyes from the afternoon sun, to scan up and down the beach for Coblaith. Her eyes lingered for a moment on the spot where she had found Angus' buttons. *Oh, Angus, we could have been friends, if'n you coulda' just given me the chance*, she thought sadly. Something made her turn, a sound from the tower, movement, a flickering. She looked up and saw Coblaith standing on the highest floor with her strange wooden tool, holding it out over the stone battlement with both hands. Her eyes were closed, and her lips were moving, but Annie could not make out the words. Some sacred Druid ritual, no doubt. "Coblaith!" she called out and raised her hand to wave.

The old woman opened her eyes and shot a disapproving stare at Annie before she disappeared within the castle.

CHAPTER TWELVE "THE CLOOTIE WELL"

That winter was hard and long. Even though they had shored up the fortress walls, the cold winds off the water were fierce and they found their way through every crack and crevice. The rooms remained drafty and damp. Conachar had his men keep fires burning night and day in the main hall to ward off the chill to no avail. When they were forced to go out to hunt and forage for food, the men came back frost-bitten and chilled to the bone. Some became sick and a few died from the fever. His entire army prayed for spring to come early and soon.

Finally, on a day when the snow had stopped falling and the ice had receded from the shoreline, when the icicles had finally melted from the eaves and windowsills, a messenger came riding up to the gate, after slogging through the mud and slush for miles, with a message from Malcom. The news was both good and bad. Malcom had slayed the usurper Macbeth in battle at Lumphanan and was marching again now that better weather prevailed. Apparently, the widow of Macbeth, Queen Graoch, was now planning to wage war against Malcom and had supplanted her own son, Lulach, on the Scottish throne. Surely now Malcom would call on Conachar and his men to follow and defend his claim to the crown! But sadly, Malcom's instructions were a staggering disappointment to him. He and his men were ordered to remain at Airchartdan, to defend it against all enemies, until he returned. Then, and only then, the letter said, would Malcom have the authority to grant the ownership of the fortress to him. In the meantime, they needed to retain control of any and all of the fortresses in Scotland.

When he read the letter to his men, the mood among them grew quickly despondent. He knew what they were feeling because it mirrored his own emotions. They had come to fight for Malcom, to bring honor and respect for the rightful Scottish king but they had for months become nothing more than carpenters and masons, caretakers to a miserable holdfast far from the battlefields, far from towns with real brothels and taverns. The few women who had remained after Malcom's departure had already been fought over and spoken for. The men that were left had no reasonable expectation of meeting any women travelling through the great glen. Conachar knew he had to do something to raise their spirits. He took his problem to the one person he knew might have a solution.

He found her alone, as always, in the catacomb, mixing herbs and berries into some mysterious potion, sitting cross-legged on the stone floor. She looked up when he entered the room and could see immediately that he was troubled.

"What ails thee, Conachar? Have your bones not yet thawed from the winter snows?"

"It is my men," he said. "We have received word from the king that we must remain in Airchartdan indefinitely. It is not sitting well with them."

The healer nodded. "No, I would expect it wouldna'. But Malcom is not yet king if what the spirits tell me is true. Macbeth is dead but his own stepson now sits on the throne. Should you not wait and see where your loyalty should be?"

"My loyalty is and always has been to Malcom, the rightful king. I was hoping he would call on us to join him now in the final battle."

"And he wants you to stay at Airchartdan?"

Conachar nodded his head sadly.

"He is right to do so. This is your home. It was the home of your ancestors. That it should be abandoned and surrendered to this new king would not be to your honor."

"But you said Macbeth had an equal claim! You said he and Malcom were both rightful heirs! Have you now taken sides in the fight?"

The woman's eyes narrowed, and she stared into his own. "You are confused who or what you owe your allegiance to. As I have told you before, I follow no king. It is you who must decide. You must figure that out for yourself."

She stood up and brushed off her long skirt. Turning her back on Conachar, she walked away haughtily without another word. Conachar's eyes followed her. She was not an *unattractive* woman. Strange, perhaps, and temperamental, but she had a certain allure about her, something tempting in a haunting sort of way. It was the fear he felt when he looked into her eyes, the power she held over him and all his men. It was as if she could see right through them to their souls, as if she could read their thoughts, their feelings and emotions. He needed her desperately, her wisdom, her knowledge of Malcom, but she scared him half to death. She seemed fearless. *How magnificent she would be on the battlefield* thought Conachar. She should fight for Malcom! Surely with her at his side, his king would be triumphant.

As the days grew warmer, the snows from the mountains melted and rushed down from the hills, rising so high the water swept over the bridge, bringing with it debris that lodged against the stone, creating a dam. Conachar's men stayed busy for days clearing it away so that the water could flow freely down into the loch. For a few days, the unwelcome orders from Malcom were forgotten, but they soon surfaced again.

He sent out hunting parties into the woods and fishing expeditions out on the water. They put up several months' worth of food and firewood, barrels of salted fish and game, cords of fodder for the great hearth. They trimmed their horses' feet and curried their manes and tails and built corrals within the palisade to house them. But, in the end, the men were dissatisfied. They drank to excess and quarreled among themselves. Conachar had to imprison the troublemakers deep in the dungeon, building an iron grate to keep them contained until they had sobered up and come to their senses. The healer was displeased. She did not want to share her underground residence with drunken prisoners. When it became unbearable, she packed up her things and returned to the woods, ignoring Conachar's pleas that he needed her to stay. He was at his wits end, a breath away from abandoning the fortress and returning to Ireland with his men. Still with no decisive battle, Malcom was becoming nothing more than a distant dream; he was just a rebel fighting for a crown on a faraway battlefield.

Then the news finally came all the way from Strathbogie in Aberdeenshire. Malcom had slain Lulach and was on his way to Scone to be crowned! The men took heart again and stopped fighting amongst themselves while they awaited the king's return to Airchartdan. Conachar himself mounted his horse and rode into the woods to find her and tell her the good news, hoping he could convince his mysterious healer, his pagan saint, to return home. He searched everywhere, every dark corner, every hidden cave, every crevice in the rocks to find her. He had to bring her home, to have her at his side when Malcom granted the fortress to him. She had made

115

it all possible and he wanted to share his good fortune with her.

He had searched for hours, and daylight was waning; the woods had grown dark and Conachar was on the verge of turning back and giving up for the day when he came upon a strange sight. There, in a low spot among the trees, invisible from the main road, he found a spring and he stopped to let his horse drink. He got down himself and dipped his hands into the cool water. It was refreshing and invigorating as it trickled down his throat and he dowsed his forehead. As he rose and looked up at the trees above, he saw it for the first time. There, hanging from all the branches were bits of clothing, hats, scarves, and rags of every sort. There were shoes hanging by their laces and shiny ribbons tied in bows, trinkets and talismans, feathers and baubles, all dangling there in the darkness. Conachar circled the tree and reached up to touch some of them and as he did, he realized this place must have been here for decades, perhaps centuries. Some of the cloth was so old it disintegrated at his touch and crumbled to the earth. Then he saw it, his own breeches, the piece bloodied by the boar, hanging there black and stiff. The wound in his leg suddenly throbbed and he remembered the pain of the tusk that had ripped it apart. He remembered, with fondness, how she had healed him, how she had come every day to his bedside and given him her strength, her rituals and omens stronger than any prayer. He looked around. This must have been her home, the source of her powers, her sanctuary from wars and men and the evil in the world.

He plunged further into the brush and finally found her in a cave, sitting against a sheer rock wall high above the Clootie Well, sitting next to a small fire. He left his horse at the foot of the cliff and climbed up the rock face, breathless for the sight of her, grinning widely when she finally came into view. "I have looked for you everywhere!" he said. "You must come back. I will never again force you to share your home with prisoners. The catacomb is yours! Malcom is finally king, and the fortress will be mine to do with as I please! It will be your home too!"

He sat down beside her near the fire and took her hands in his. Her shawl fell from her shoulder and for the first time he noticed the paintings on her upper arm. Strange, Pictish symbols, scratched, embedded in her otherwise lovely flesh. Had she done this because of him? Had she inflicted pain upon herself at losing her home? Tears welled in his eyes as he looked deeply into hers.

"Will you come home with me? Back to Airchartdan? Back to your home?"

"What need have you of me now? Your king is on the throne. Your men will stop fighting amongst themselves. What need have you for an old woman?"

It was a strange thing to say. He stared at her. "*Old* woman? But you are not old! You are young and beautiful. More beautiful than any woman in the world!"

His compliment brought the inkling of a smile to her face.

"Say you will come!" he begged.

She pulled her hands away and reached down to kindle the fire. The flames danced in her eyes and smoldered across her hair creating a halo-like glow around her face. For several long moments she said not a word. She raised her arm, letting her hand rest upon the stone wall of the cave and closed her eyes. Conachar watched her in hypnotized curiosity.

"They are on their way now," she said almost in a whisper. "Feel them, Conachar."

117

She took his hand and placed it against the wall next to her own. Once again, he could feel the vibrations in the stone, the rumbling of horses' hooves, the slapping of metal against leather, the faraway voices of soldiers. He pulled his hand away.

"Malcom will be here soon," she said, "and with him, hundreds of men and horses. Airchartdan will be his home for a time and then he will be gone. You were meant to rule Airchartdan, and you will remain."

Conachar felt his spirit sink. "Do you mean I will always be just a *caretaker*? He will never need me to fight alongside him in battle?"

"The battles are over for a time," she said simply. "Malcom will not live forever. There will be other kings on the Scottish throne."

"Who?" he demanded to know. "Who will dare to unseat my king?"

At that she laughed heartily. "You are such a child. So naïve and innocent. No king can live forever. Your Malcom will rule for a time. Then there will be others. Bane, another Duncan, Edgar…."

Conachar stared at her. "Where will *I* be then?"

"You will be dead."

Her words shocked him. She spoke so bluntly, never softening the blows her words wielded.

"There will be others too. Invaders from the south who speak a foreign tongue. *Normans* they will call themselves."

It was too much to take in and understand for Conachar. Seeing into the future was beyond his comprehension. He only wanted to stay in the present, basking in the triumph and glory of Malcom's victory. He didn't want to know that one day another king would take the crown, that one day he would be dead and buried.

"I do not want Malcom to die."

"All men must die, Conachar. It is our destiny."

He laid his head across her lap then and curled his legs up to his chest as she stroked his hair and began to sing softly. He closed his eyes and let her lilting voice drift through his brain, the touch of her fingers creating a strange sensation on his scalp. For years he had longed desperately for a woman's love, settling for the fleeting affections of the Drumnadrochit whores that could be purchased with a silver coin. "Say you will come home with me," he murmured like a child.

"When Malcom and his army have departed, I will return."

"And may I stay here with you tonight?"

"Aye."

There was a pause.

"I am afraid of dying," confessed Conachar.

"We all have to die sometime," said the healer. "I have died many times. Death is nothing to fear."

CHAPTER THIRTEEN "CURSED"

Annie had not wanted to venture outside at all that day. It was bitterly cold and the winds off the water were like sharp needles pricking her face when she had peeked out from the stairs above earlier that morning. But Coblaith insisted they needed to gather the last of the winter berries from the woods and had sent her off with an empty sack.

"What will *you* be doing while I am freezing in the woods?" she asked.

"Foraging for food, just as you are," said Coblaith. "Do you think I am idle just because you cannot see what I am doing? I told you when you first became an orphan that I would not allow you to lord over me. Now, off with ya, before I change my mind and you will be livin' elsewhere."

Annie smiled. Coblaith reminded her of Olin, when she scolded and chided her and pretended to be angry. She knew, just as she had with the wizard, that the old woman was growing fond of her, that they needed each other to survive, especially in the dead of winter. Her threats were empty. "Well, I hope you bag a nice fat partridge, or, better yet, a chicken from one of the coops in Drumnadrochit. I saw some when I was there that would make a juicy stew."

"I'm no thief," replied Coblaith haughtily.

Annie laughed as she climbed the stairs, flinging her bag over her shoulder. "I will be back by suppertime."

The wind struck her the moment she stepped outside the castle, blowing her skirt high above her knees and biting at her legs. She wished she had learned the art of knitting. A warm mask to cover her face and woolen stockings on days like these would come in handy. As it was her winter clothing was becoming increasingly inadequate. Deidre's old skirt by itself was too thin for winter, so she wore it over her old stained one; her shoes had holes in the soles and her stockings were ragged and run. If only she could sew herself a wardrobe from her forest gleanings, from the bark and leaves and bushes. If only she had cloth or wool to work with! Coblaith never seemed to get cold, and her clothing was no thicker or warmer than her own. And they were both so thin, existing on bannocks and berries and fish when they could catch them. Now that winter was in full blast, the fish were sleeping deep in the loch, in the warm peat valleys and vales beneath the surface of the water. While the loch was too deep to freeze completely, ice encroached all along the shoreline like a thick white mantel.

Even the sun was cold that day, shining down on her shoulders like a frozen spear, glaring and reflecting off the snowy landscape, blinding her. Annie hurried up the road, now deep with snow, sinking to her shins and shivering all the way. If she had known she would be foraging in the wintertime she would have planted vegetables in the castle garden. She was growing tired of nettle soup and dandelion salad. If the Ceardannan had not deserted her, she would be sharing venison stew with Deidre and Geoffrey around the fire. It would still be cold, but her gut would be full and warm.

The castle had lost its original fascination for Annie. Even with Coblaith for company, she felt isolated from the world outside. The stone walls protected her from the cold, but they did not speak to her as they did to Coblaith. The people of Drumnadrochit were unfriendly. Few, if any, travelers passed by on the road to visit with. Wars were being won and lost out there somewhere. Whether her brothers were alive or dead she might never know. Sometimes, the loneliness she felt sunk into her bones and made them ache. *Was this what a broken heart felt like*? she often wondered.

Good fortune was on her side that day, however. Even though she had hiked deeper into the woods than she had been since the day the Ceardannan had traveled through it from Cromarty, she finally found a patch of berry bushes tucked away from the main road, out of sight, overlooked by the pickers from town. She quickly ran through them, plucking and bagging them with her frost-bitten fingers, sucking the juice away and savoring the tartness on her tongue. When she had stripped the last cluster she perused even deeper into the woods, hoping to impress Coblaith with a full sack on her return.

It was then that she saw it. A small spring that had somehow remained unfrozen in the middle of the snow and above it, in a tree, hundreds, perhaps thousands, of oddities, garments, rags, and trinkets hanging frozen and coated with white. *What was this place?* Annie wondered. Who had put all these things here? Things they could use! Valuable things! Pieces of cloth to sew a new skirt for her, warm mittens to keep her hands from freezing, leather to repair the soles of her shoes. She began to pull the items down, everything she could reach, stuffing them into her sack along with the berries until it was full to the brim and almost too heavy to carry. Wouldn't Coblaith be pleased? More treasures for her sea chest! Perhaps things they could barter for other things they needed.

She flung the bag over her shoulder and started back toward the castle, following her own footsteps in the snow. When she reached the edge of the woods and stepped out into the bright sunlight, her eyes were blinded by the glare. She closed and shielded her eyes, blinking them slowly open. She squinted, thinking she must be seeing things. People! Men! Soldiers!

Marching down the road toward her, the sound of pipes, shrill against the empty silence of the day. She studied them. They were not English soldiers, no red coats, no English flag waving. These men were wearing kilts and white roses on their bonnets! These were Jacobites! Maybe Alex had returned to her!

She dropped the bag at her feet and stepped aside to let them pass. Some of the men smiled at her; some bowed their heads. But they kept moving, no time to stop for a young girl alongside the road. They were on their way to war. No time to waste in conversation.

"Excuse me, Sir," she called out to one of them, any one of them, she didn't care which one. "Where is it you are going?"

One man paused and broke out of line. He approached her and bowed to her politely. "Why, we are off to Inverness, Lassie. But why are you out here all alone on this wintry day? You should be inside by a fire. You'll take your death out here!"

"I will be by a fire very soon, Sir," said Annie. "What is in Inverness? Is that where your army is camped? My brother marched off with the Jacobites months ago and I havna' heard from him since. I would like to send word to him if'n I could."

The man smiled. "Your brother is one of us then! What is his name, Lassie? If'n I see him I will pass along your message."

"Alex. Alex Urquhart, Sir. Please tell him his little sister waits for his return. I'll be here at the castle until he comes."

Turning, the man looked at the castle and then back at Annie. "You are living in those old ruins, Lassie? All by yourself?"

"No, I am not all alone. I have a friend. An old Druid woman stays with me. We are quite safe, I assure you."

He shook his head. "Aye? Well, take care the English army doesna' find you. And dinnae' tell anyone your brother is a Jacobite. They'll string you up for sure!"

"I willna'," Annie replied. "But you will tell my brother if'n you see him? Promise?"

The soldier laughed and got back into line.

"I promise you I will, Lassie!"

He joined the others and they marched off into the woods leaving a wide trail in the snow. Annie's heart ached at watching them go. She resisted the urge to follow them and hoisted her heavy bag up over her shoulder, hurrying down the hill toward the castle, eager to show Coblaith the treasures she had found. Her chance meeting with the Jacobites had given her new hope that her brother would return.

The old woman was seated by the fire in the catacomb, skewering a fish on a spit of wood to roast it, scraping away its shiny scales with a knife. She looked up as Annie burst into the room and flung the heavy bag down on the stone floor.

"Wait until you see what I have found!" She opened the bag and put the bunches of winter berries aside before she began spreading her cache of trinkets out in front of the fire. "Look, Coblaith! Cloth to sew with, mittens and socks to warm our feet, leather to repair our worn-out shoes!"

Coblaith stared at the array of items before her. Her face took on an angry scowl and her eyes pinched together as if she could not believe what she was seeing. She reached out and picked up a piece of cloth and squeezed it in her hand. Shaking her head, she began to breathe deeply as if to calm her rage. She closed her eyes and bit her lip in silence for several moments before she spoke.

"You have stolen these from the Clootie Well."

Annie shrugged. "If that is what you call it. Some kind travelers left all these useful things hanging in a tree! Things we can use! I just happened to come across it while I was searching for berries! Is it not wonderful, Coblaith?"

Annie watched as the woman began rocking back and forth. An eerie moan came from her throat. Her eyes opened suddenly and out of her mouth spit words like venom. "Do you not realize what you have done? We are surely cursed now! I always knew you were a stupid girl, but this is far worse."

"What? What have I done? Someone left these gifts in the woods for me to find. Your gods or spirits or whatever you call them must be watching over us! It was only by good fortune…."

"Good fortune? Have you gone mad? You have stolen all the blessings there! You have brought evil down upon our heads! These were sacred offerings! Would you steal alms from a church altar? Would you rob a grave? Would you wish to take away blessings from those who need it most?"

Annie was confused. She did not realize that the strange things she had found hanging in the tree were of a spiritual value. They were just old junk someone had left there. How was she to know they had some hidden meaning? Some religious connotations? She opened her mouth to speak but the expression on Coblaith's face muted her. She shook her head and dropped her shoulders, letting out her disappointment with a deep sigh. "I'm sorry," she mumbled. "I didna' know."

Coblaith stood up abruptly. She began gathering up all the items, stuffing them back into her bag before she swung the bag around and positioned it on her shoulder. "I must try to reverse the evil you have done."

She hurried up the stairwell, leaving Annie speechless and alone by the fire. Annie reached out and turned the fish over so it would not burn although she had lost her appetite for food. She hungered for understanding, for knowledge. No one had ever taken the time to teach her such things. Druid laws were beyond her comprehension. Coblaith never completely explained any of the rituals she performed. Why was she not warned that there were blessings and curses and strange trees with magical powers in the woods? She would not have touched them if she had known! How could ignorance be a curse? It was all Coblaith's fault…. if she had only explained it to her.

The fish began to sizzle. It was done. Annie removed it from the fire, resting it on a wooden trencher. Still not hungry, she wandered off to her bed and pulled the blankets over her shoulders. She had never seen Coblaith so angry, and she was fearful what would happen when she returned. Would she banish her from the castle? Would she force her out into the snow in the dead of winter? If that happened, where would she go? She wasn't sure she could make it all the way to Inverness alone. She knew she was not welcome in Drumnadrochit. She wished she could go to sleep and wake up back in Cromarty, back in her warm bed in the little house on Bank Street, seeing her brothers off to work on the docks but those days were gone.

She drowsed, the crackling of the fire making soft music in her ears. She would sleep and all would make sense in the morning, when Coblaith returned, *if* she returned. Surely all would be well in the morning.

CHAPTER FOURTEEN "RETURN OF THE KING"

Malcom had finally returned. His personal army, with conscripts supplied by the English king Edward the Confessor and Northumbrian soldiers led by General Siward, rode through the glen by the hundreds and landed dozens of ships for miles up and down the shore around Airchartdan. Over the course of a day, the fortress was suddenly overrun with soldiers and horses. Wagons of supplies rumbled across the bridge and female camp followers were not far behind. Bards and minstrels and pipers playing and shepherds with herds of sheep passed through the gate, taking up residence within the palisade. Observing all the commotion in the courtyard from his bedchamber window, Conachar hurried to dress in his best tunic and polished his sword before he made his way out to welcome the newly crowned king.

They greeted one another with a warm embrace. Malcom was surprised and pleased with the renovations Conachar had made to the fortress. His eyes took in every detail from the interior buildings to the strong rock wall surrounding them, the stables, the kitchens, the grand hall. They knelt side by side in the little chapel to give thanks for a successful campaign. "I could not have left Airchartdan in more able hands," the king whispered in Conachar's ear, planting a kiss on the top of his head. "Your loyalty will be rewarded!"

Trees were felled and brought in from the woods. A great fire was lit while sheep were slaughtered and butchered for the celebration. By sunset the aroma of roasting mutton and yeasty ale filled the air as spits were turned over glowing coals and barrels were tapped and emptied. For the first time music could be heard within the walls and drifted out over the water in joyous melodies. It was a night like the old fortress had never seen before and would never see again.

Malcom gathered his most trusted men around him. The general and his captains were at his right hand at the long trestles set up in the great hall. Conachar and his men were on the king's left. They all ate and drank heartily until late into the night before they finally wandered off to sleep in the corners and crannies of the fortress. By morning the courtyard looked as if the war had been fought right there at Airchartdan, littered with empty tankards and used trenchers, chewed bones and breadcrusts, strewn amid the sleeping soldiers. As sunlight crept over the wall and the men began to awaken and move about, more barrels of ale were opened to relieve their aching heads. Women rose and rekindled the fire for morning bannocks to be made by the hundreds.

That afternoon the king walked to the top of the grassy motte with his longsword in hand. He ordered his men to form a semi-circle and directed Conachar to kneel at his feet. When he spoke, the entire courtyard fell silent.

"As newly crowned King of Scotland, I hereby grant the fortress of Airchartdan to my loyal servant and soldier, Conachar, of the Royal House of Ulster, for his use and residence from this day forward, and for his sons and grandsons to follow him, in perpetuity." He raised his sword and gently tapped Conachar on each shoulder and then planted the blade in the ground. They embraced again and the celebrations began all over again. Another night of eating and drinking followed, and another, until a week had passed. It was then the king got back to business and made known his intentions for the fortress.

"I have seen many holdfasts destroyed in the battles I have fought against Macbeth. New weapons that wield fire are our biggest threat."

Conachar listened intently, eager to please the man who had honored him. "That is why I built you a strong palisade, my king."

"The fortress must also be rebuilt in stone. Wood will burn and can be destroyed by our enemies."

"What enemies do you speak of?"

Conachar believed that there would be peace in Scotland now that Macbeth and Lulach were dead. Who would challenge the king now?

"We have invaders from the north," replied the king. "Northmen and Danes. Pirates who are sacking our villages and towns all along our eastern border. They have attacked Ireland too, even the sacred island of Iona where they have massacred the monks and set fire to the monastery." He paused, as if in deep thought. "And no king can expect to go unchallenged forever. Eventually, there will be those who wish to take my crown away."

"Airchartdan has no wealth for them to steal. We have no gold or silver relics of value. We are just a pile of stones at the edge of a lake. What could they possibly want with us?"

The king had gained knowledge from the wars. He was a wiser and more worldly man than he had been before. "They are coming to Scotland and Ireland and England to live, to settle and make their homes. They are bringing their women and children and building their own villages. A fortress such as Airchartdan would be a strategic place for them with good grazing land and ample woods and access to the loch for their ships. We must be prepared to defend it."

At that moment, Conachar realized he could be tied to Airchartdan indefinitely, to hold it for Malcom, for *Scotland.*

The king remained over the summer months, to assist Conachar in shoring up the walls of Airchartdan. He sent his men out on ships and wagons to gather stones in great quantities and they built scaffolds all around the main fortress from which to work. The soldiers who were experienced in masonry were put to the task of covering everything that was vulnerable to fire with stone and mortar. The palisade wall was heightened to make it tall enough to be difficult to scale from the outside; they installed a strong iron portcullis at the gate. By the time Malcom and his army were prepared to move on to his home in Fife and his ships began to sail north the courtyard at Airchartdan became empty and quiet again. Conachar felt the first pangs of loneliness begin to set in. The excitement of having the king in residence, the monumental task of building the walls and housing hundreds of men had kept his mind off matters of his heart. The first night after Malcom had left, the newly appointed *laird* of Airchartdan stood alone in his bedchamber, peering out over the black water, thinking of the woman who had saved him from death, who had given his life purpose, of meaning. The woman who had been the first to stir emotion in him. He thought of her, miles away in her cave in the woods, remembering their last night together and realized how desperately he needed her now.

At dawn, he saddled his horse and rode through the gate and over the bridge at a quick trot. He declined when his men suggested they accompany him for protection. After all, he was now *nobility* and noblemen always had guards at their sides, but this was something he needed to do alone.

He urged his horse to a gallop in the woods, treading softly and quickly over the soft cushioned path. As he drew near to the Clootie Well, where he tied up his horse, his heart began to flutter with anticipation.

He climbed the face of the rock, one foot at a time, slowly and silently, preparing to surprise her with his good news before he realized she probably already knew what he was going to tell her. How could he forget that she had powers of sight, into the future, into the past? He climbed upward and finally reached the mouth of the cave and stepped inside, adjusting his eyes to the darkness. There was no fire, only a single torch hanging from the rock wall. Beneath it he saw her, sitting cross-legged as was her usual pose, her head down, holding a small bundle in her arms. At the sound of his footfall, she looked up and smiled.

"Conachar," she said simply. "You have returned."

He stepped forward, staring at her. Her sleeve was pulled down, her bare shoulder exposed. There, at her breast was a baby suckling contentedly. Conachar's mouth fell open and he audibly gasped at the sight. He fell to his knees and reached out to touch her face; his eyes dropped to the babe in her arms. He could not find words. His mouth was dry and his lips limp in awe. Finally, it was she who broke the silence.

"Your son," she said simply and without emotion.

"My.... *son*...??"

"I have named him William Urquhart."

The name had no meaning to Conachar. Some Gaelic name.

"Urquhart?"

"It means *of the forest*," she explained. "For that is where he was born."

Conachar reached out and took the infant boy in his sturdy hands and raised him up in the light to get a better look.

"He has my red face. And he is good and heavy!"

His mother smiled. "Aye, he was a pain to bring into the world."

"I did not know. I would have come earlier."

"You had a king to serve," she said. "And now you have Airchartdan."

Conachar shook his head.

"Airchartdan is nothing but a holdfast. *Now I have a son!*"

CHAPTER FIFTEEN
"IMPRISONED"

When Annie opened her eyes the next morning, the embers in the firepit were lying beside her like a nest of molten eggs but the air in the catacomb was heavy and damp. She immediately filled the firepit with dried leaves to rekindle the flame. *Would winter ever be over?* she wondered sourly. The stones were still warm from the fire. Reaching for a cold bannock she heated it on them and stared at the empty place where Coblaith usually sat. Her bed was empty and unslept in. Annie felt guilt like a heavy chain around her heart. If only she hadn't stolen those things from the Clootie Well! If only she had known...

She crawled back beneath her blanket to keep warm, but she could not go back to sleep. She had to go and search for her, to apologize and beg the old woman's forgiveness. The thought of living alone in the castle now seemed unbearable. She pulled on her shoes after stuffing leaves in them to cover the holes where the soles had worn through and wrapped her blanket around her shoulders, knotting it across her breast like a shawl, stretching her hands one more time over the fire for warmth.

The day was cloudy and grey outside. As she stepped into the courtyard, now covered in pristine white snow, she watched her breath rise before her, disappearing into the cold air. Her feet crunched as if she were stepping on gravel as she headed through the gatehouse and the bridge was slippery with ice, so she tiptoed warily along, balancing herself against the rock wall. The toads were long buried in the riverbank for the winter. She would not see them again until the spring. *Even the toads had abandoned her!*

When she reached the road and turned toward the woods, she noticed the footprints stretching out ahead of her, a trail of many feet. She had heard nothing in the night, nothing since the dawn. How could so many people have passed, and she not hear them? Could it be more Jacobites, heading off to Inverness? The thought of that cheered her momentarily. It made her feel closer to Alex. She had already begun to plan what she would do if Coblaith did not return; she would walk to Inverness, following the road she knew led there, back to the ferry landing, back to the only place she knew to look for him. Damn the snow and ice! She would go back to the Clootie Well and steal what she pleased from it to protect her feet and her body from the cold, and she would walk until she got there. No one could stop her. She knew the way. If the war was over and Alex was coming for her, perhaps they would meet on the road. She had it all plotted out in her head.

The snow was not as deep under the trees and she avoided the drifts as much as possible, saving her feet which had already grown numb. Without the sun above, the woods grew darker and more ominous. The footprints marched silently before her; she was counting them now. Two, three, four men perhaps, marching down the path. Not enough to be an army. Maybe hunters looking for boar or deer. Whoever they were, she hoped they would not be hostile. She would play the damsel who had lost her way and not reveal the fact that her brother was a Jacobite or that her family were once members of the hated Ceardannan. They would not know who she was if she kept quiet about it. Come to think of it even *she* wasn't sure who she was anymore!

The sound of voices broke the silence ahead of her and she suddenly was afraid. She darted into the underbrush and hid behind the snow-covered branches as the voices got closer. Men, three or four, she estimated. She narrowed her eyes and parted the branches to see who they were. Three men, in heavy coats and hats, dragging something behind them. A deer perhaps or a boar? No, it was a person in a white cloak with white hair, with hands trussed together; the men's voices grew louder so she could hear what they were saying.

"Take her back to that cursed castle," said one voice.

"We should burn her at the stake," said another.

"Rid the place of witches once and for all!"

Annie gasped audibly. Her hand flew to her mouth to muffle the sound. Thankfully the men's footsteps and conversation had blotted out her utterance. She watched them pass, poor Coblaith stumbling along, falling to her knees and being jerked roughly back to her feet by her captors. One of them reached out and pulled her by the hair and the old woman cried out in pain. Annie 's mind was racing. No longer were her thoughts on returning to Inverness to find Alex. Now she had to do something to help Coblaith! But what could she do against three strong men? She watched them emerge from the woods onto the snowy road before she came out of the bushes and followed them.

She watched them cross the bridge and disappear into the courtyard. Their feet had trampled the ice on the stones, so she began to run without fear of falling, desperately trying to do something to save the only friend she had in the world! She halted in the doorway of the gatehouse, lingering in the shadow of the stone pillars to watch. The men had thrown Coblaith down on the snow, and one held her down with his foot while the others were carrying on a serious conversation.

"We cannae' just burn her without a trial," one was saying. "That would be murder!"

"Ain't no such thing as *murderin'* a witch. The church will bless us fer it!"

The man whose foot was planted in the middle of Coblaith's back rubbed his chin. "We should lock her up fer now and talk to the priest. He'll know how we should handle it. Getting' rid of devils is *his* work!"

"But we cannae' take her back to Drumnadrochit! She could put a curse on the entire town! We should leave her here in the castle. Tie her up a 'course, where she cannae' escape."

It was decided. Annie sunk back out of sight as they dragged poor Coblaith toward the tower and down the stairs to the catacomb. When they had disappeared, she stepped out and ran to the stairwell, silently tiptoeing down a few steps, listening to the men, concealing herself in the last spiral of the stair. She could see them standing over the iron grate. One of the men cursed when he discovered the lock.

"Who has a key to this?" he was asking Coblaith. "You?"

No, no, no…. Annie was thinking…. *dinnae' tell them! Dinnae' give them the key!*

She could not believe her ears when the old woman answered, "I do. Here. Lock me away if it suits you. I dinnae' fear the stones of this place."

She watched as Coblaith dug into her pocket and handed the skeleton key to him.

How could she be so stupid?

The man took the key and inserted it into the lock, flinging the grate open with a loud bang. He got down on his knees and strained his eyes to see inside. "Nothin' down here but water and rock. She couldna' escape. We will just lock her up while we go see the priest."

He then grabbed Coblaith and shoved her down through the hole. Annie could not contain herself any longer. She jumped up and bounded down the remaining steps to confront the men.

"Stop! You cannae' lock her away! She is no witch! She is only a gentle Druid!"

All three men turned and stared at Annie, eyes agog and mouths open.

"Where did *you* come from?" said one, as he came forward and took Annie roughly by the arm. "How many of you are there in this place? Maybe we should burn the whole castle down and be done with the lot of you!"

While one man unlocked the grate again, another pushed Annie down after Coblaith. She tumbled head over heels and landed hard on the stone ledge. The sound of the lock clicked in her brain, and she panicked. Standing up she gripped the iron slats and shook them. "You cannae lock us down here! We are not witches! We have done nothing wrong!"

"You can convince the priest of that after we tell him of your magic tree in the woods, of your fires in the night and your pagan rituals. Who else but witches would live in this place?"

They turned and left them then, disappearing up the stairwell, their footsteps fading away in the snowy landscape outside. Annie heard Coblaith rummaging around in her old sea chest. A moment later she heard the distinct scrape of a flint against stone and the flicker of a flame on a torch. Out of the darkness the old woman's face appeared, scratched and bruised and broken.

"Coblaith! Are you hurt very badly? Did they beat you?"

The old woman shrugged. "I've had worse."

"What will we do now? Why *ever* did you give them the key to this place? Now we are trapped forever until they come to burn the castle down. Unless…. you have another key?"

The old woman was silent.

"Talk to me, Coblaith! I am sorry for what I did. I will never do it again! Please forgive me! Were you able to put back all the blessings at the Clootie Well?"

Coblaith nodded. She settled herself against the rock wall and rested her head.

Annie dropped down and sat beside her, heaving a deep sigh of hopelessness. "I guess we will both die here in this place."

"No. We just have to wait on the moon." Coblaith pulled another blanket from the sea chest and offered it to Annie.

Annie pulled her own blanket from around her shoulders. "You take that one. I have mine," she said as she unfolded it and wrapped it around herself.

Coblaith extinguished the torch, tamping and rolling it against the rock until the flame went out. She positioned herself between the ledge and the rock wall, rolling up like a caterpillar in a cocoon.

"I cannae' sleep now, wondering if those men will return. They want to burn us at the stake! How can you sleep when our lives are in danger?"

Coblaith rolled over, turning her face against the wall; Annie could not see her but could hear her movements.

"Why, pray tell, do we have to wait on the moon? What has the moon got to do with it? And how will we know when the moon has risen anyway? We cannae' even see the sky from inside this cave!"

Coblaith sighed. Silently, she reached over and patted Annie's shoulder. "Ya will have to trust me, Lassie."

Annie reached up and put her hands on the wall. She had watched Coblaith do it many times. The old woman said the walls spoke to her. At first, the stone beneath her palm was cold and clammy. Then, strangely, it began to warm to her touch, like a door opening to sunlight, like a window welcoming in a summer breeze. She felt the warmth spread up her arm and drape itself across her shoulders, like a soft fur cloak.

"Coblaith! I can feel it! I can feel the walls communicating with me but I cannae' understand them."

Annie heard the old woman groan again in the darkness.

"Cannae' you hear what they are saying?"

Coblaith rolled over a second time. "They are saying, *be quiet and go to sleep.*"

CHAPTER SIXTEEN "MARCH OF THE KINGS"

Young William thrived at Airchartdan. Almost as soon as he was able to walk Conachar began teaching the boy to hold a sword and mace, to hunt and fish, to ride a horse, everything he thought a man needed to know in life. While the boy's mother went back to the catacomb beneath the fortress to live, the boy was given a bedchamber upstairs, next to his own, with a comfortable bed and a fireplace to keep him warm at night. He always kept the boy near him during the day. Before he went to bed himself every night, he would check on the sleeping youngster, tuck the blankets around him and stoke the fire in his room. Conachar's world had evolved from being a soldier to being a doting father. It consumed him completely, often to the dereliction of his other duties.

Years passed. The boy soon grew taller than his father by a foot; his shoulders were broader by several inches. He had Conachar's hair and his mother's eyes and a gentle demeanor like the woman who gave birth to him. Early on, he took to the back of a horse as if his body was a continuing appendage of the four-legged creature he sat upon. He developed an ease of movement, a fluidity, a natural confluence of muscle and bone as if the horse's legs were extensions of his own. The horse's ears tilted backward so they were constantly in communication with each other. They were one, like a Greek centaur, speaking the same language, a talent Conachar conceded came from the boy's mother.

When they first began his training with the sword, Conachar had the castle smithy craft a smaller blade, lighter and easier for the boy to handle. Sparring with his father, with his small, round shield, the boy was light on his feet and extremely agile, more than Conachar had ever been himself. Hunting proved to be more of a challenge. Young William consistently hesitated too long to take a shot with his bow, frequently giving his prey ample time to run away. Conachar suspected it was his kind spirit that was holding him back.

"I have no qualms about defending myself in battle, Da," William told him. "But the deer has done me no harm."

"That is your mother talking," barked Conachar. "We need to eat, Boy! You cannot live without food."

"I know you are right," William replied with a shrug. "I'm sorry."

Conachar felt guilty criticizing the boy's mother. "She is a kind soul, William. She is one with the earth and the animals who live upon it. As men, we cannot afford such tender feelings."

"It is more than that, Father. It is true she has compassion for all life, from the trees in the great glen to the fish that swim in the loch to the *clan a cheo*. She believes man must take little and give back much. The stones say…."

"Stones do not speak! That is where your mother and I disagree! I'll hear no more of it!"

They ended the lesson abruptly and Conachar did not force the boy to accompany him on hunts after that, concentrating on his sword skills instead.

The king seldom visited Airchartdan after that. Conachar received news from the east periodically, telling of the king's marriage to an English princess, of skirmishes with the Gaelic tribes. Then came news of another military invasion, not from the Danes but from the south by a horde from Francia who called themselves Normans, just as the healer had predicted. England seemed far away, however, and Conachar did not

141

worry about it too much, but it kept the king occupied for years. Conachar's focus was on the boy and his education. He needed to grow up strong to defend Airchartdan against invasion.

The boy's relationship with his mother was strange from the start. While the boy was fascinated with the woman who gave life to him and the strange cave in which she lived, Conachar would only allow him occasional visits and only in his presence. Young William learned from her an entirely different curriculum than his father was teaching him. From her he learned about the spirits in animals and birds, about the legends of the loch, about the Clootie Well, *and he learned to listen to the stones.*

"You must not believe everything your mother tells you," Conachar told him every time they would return to the above-ground world. "She lives in a world that is very different than we do."

"Is she mad?" the boy asked.

"No, not mad exactly. She just has a vivid imagination."

Conachar was afraid to tell the boy how his mother had saved his own life and helped him through difficult times. He feared that the boy would become too immersed in her Druidic lifestyle, that his young mind was too impressionable.

Malcom III had now ruled Scotland for many years and for a time managed to protect the north and south from invaders. When he finally died, the crown was passed to a succession of petty kings, none of whom held it for very long. The stone of Scone barely had a chance to grow cold with the many knees that had knelt upon it. Airchartdan became a vacation destination for them, particularly in the summers when the weather was warm. They would come with their entourages to

142

hunt in the woods and fish in the loch, staying for weeks and sometimes months, all the while depleting the stores of food and fuel that Conachar had worked to build. He began to resent them for turning his military fortress into a royal retreat. It was not until a new king called William the Lion, the great grandson of Malcom III, came to visit that everything changed for Conachar.

The new king was greatly impressed by the thick walls and strong iron gates, by the forges and kilns Conachar had built to make weaponry, by the fine warhorses raised in his stables. "You must build me more castles like this!" he told the elderly Irishman who was now content to live out the rest of his life in his own home.

"I am too old to build another like Airchartdan," Conachar replied. "I am afraid I have given all my useful years to this place. Building another would surely kill me."

King William would not take no for an answer. "Your son then!" He turned to the boy. "Can you build a castle like this for me?"

Conachar was afraid the king would take his son away. "He is still a boy, my king. I have raised him to be a soldier, not a mason! He has no skills…."

"I can supply the masons and carpenters. He knows this place inside and out. I just need him to design it and supervise the construction."

It was not a casual request the king was making; it was a *royal command*. Conachar had no choice but to agree. And so it was that young William kissed his mother goodbye and embraced his father before he rode off that summer day with the king and his men to a place called Cromarty on the Black Isle to build a castle there.

CHAPTER SEVENTEEN
"ESCAPE"

Annie was sitting beside Coblaith in the frigid cave. With nothing left with which to build a fire and having eaten the last of their small cache of food, their chances of starving to death before they were burned as witches was becoming more than likely. The men still had not returned from Drumnadrochit as if they had been forgotten. Their savior was a welcome blizzard that had blown down from the highlands overnight and for a time it provided a deep white barrier of protection for the two prisoners in the castle dungeon. In the dying flame of their only torch Annie watched as the old woman took her strange, forked tool out and held it out over the black water at their feet.

"What are you doing?" she asked. "You have never told me what that piece of wood is for."

Coblaith had closed her eyes, as if in a trance, and did not answer. Annie watched the branch in her shivering hands in awe, waiting for something magical to happen. The ritual went on for a long time before the branch suddenly dipped low and appeared to shudder. Bubbles appeared on the water. Coblaith opened her eyes and smiled. "It is time," she said, "but we must hurry. Take your blanket and roll it up tightly. You will have to hold it on your head to keep it dry."

"It is dry now," said Annie. "Why must I hold it on my head?"

"Just do as I say," replied Coblaith with irritation in her voice.

The old woman clutched her own blanket and positioned it on her head with one hand. She sat on her haunches like a hare ready to pounce at the very edge of the precipice above the water, watching the surface intently. "Get ready."

Annie was losing patience. "Get ready for *what*? Coblaith will you kindly tell me what it is you are talking aboot. What is happening? Do you hear something in the walls?"

Suddenly, a sliver of light appeared on the surface of the water, growing wider and brighter, creeping slowly all the way toward the ledge where they sat, revealing an opening to the outside world. Annie could see daylight coming through! Coblaith jumped down, still holding her blanket on her head with one hand while treading toward the light with the other. She shrieked when the cold water first touched her skin.

"What are you doing? You will freeze to death!"

"Follow me, silly girl. It is our only way out. We must get out while the tide is low for it will return soon and imprison us again."

Annie was beginning to understand. They had been waiting on the moon for the tide to shift in the loch and reveal an opening in the cave. Before she could jump in after Coblaith, however, the bats awakened and came fluttering down from the ceiling, their wings flapping and snapping, their tongues clicking out a strange language only they could understand. The noise was deafening as they flew toward the spot of light and out into the air outside. They passed over Coblaith's head and out over the water like a thick black cloud and within minutes were gone from sight. Annie looked upward to be sure the last of them had departed before she slid herself off the ledge into the icy pool.

It took her by surprise. The cold was like a knife stabbing through her chest, her abdomen. Her extremities felt numb, all her senses lost in the frozen abyss. She could hardly breathe.

"Come now, Lassie. Follow me. Keep your blanket out of the water. You're g'wine to need it."

Annie gulped for air and positioned her folded blanket on her head, although she couldn't feel her fingers. Her feet somehow managed to move forward. They waded then, up to their shoulders, through the water, toward the light. "Didna' ya say this was once a prison?"

"Aye," replied Coblaith, "just not a very good one."

Annie wanted to laugh but it hurt too much. When they had reached the outside of the cave and Annie could see the shoreline beneath the castle, her heart began to pump wildly. Taking long strides toward the beach with unfeeling legs beneath her she followed Coblaith. One more foot, one more inch, one more moment in the icy water seemed like it took an eternity. The air was nearly as cold as the water and her nostrils burned with every breath, but the sunshine on her face urged her onward. Coblaith climbed up on the bank ahead of her and turned to help the girl. Their teeth were chattering in unison; their entire bodies trembling and convulsing. Without hesitation they both dropped their wet clothes on the sand and wrapped their naked bodies up in their blankets. Annie's feet hurt so badly she was afraid she would be unable to walk.

"We need to run," said Coblaith, "to get the blood pumping in your feet. Now!"

And off they ran, through the trees, stumbling toward the woods. The snow had blown in from the north and surrounded them in drifts and banks, but they were able to circle the deepest parts and reach the trees where the ground was not so cold. Annie hadn't the time to think about the pain. When they finally reached the Clootie Well, their eyes fell upon the tree, now chopped to the ground, lying in a heap of broken

146

branches on the forest floor, the fallen trinkets laced with ice and dusted with snow. They hadn't time to mourn its passing. Their frozen bodies needed warmth to stay alive.

"Where are we going?" Annie's stuttered her words from blue lips.

Coblaith did not answer. She turned away from the tree and ran off into the thick underbrush. Annie followed until they reached a strange rock formation jutting out of the ground hidden behind the trees. She began to climb up the face of it that was now slippery with ice. Annie climbed a few steps behind her without questioning it. She was no longer afraid of death for nothing could have been more terrifying than the cold water and running through the snow with wet feet. She ached all over and her head felt like it was about to burst from the pain. They climbed upward until they reached the mouth of a small cave, hidden away in the stones.

The old woman entered it and looked around as if she had been there before; there was a blackened firepit and there were animal furs and wool blankets lying nearby. She hurried toward a tinder and kindling pile in a corner. She found a flint and struck it against the stone wall to light a fire.

Annie fell to her knees beside the tiny flame, burying her arms deeper into the folds of her blanket, wiggling her fingers and rubbing her toes to be sure they had not fallen off in the cold. Coblaith adjusted her own blanket and sat down across the fire from the girl, adding another piece of wood and another and another until they could feel the heat begin to warm their faces. Annie reached down and pulled off her wet shoes.

"Here, try these," said Coblaith, handing her a pair of wool stockings. "Put your shoes near the fire to dry."

Annie looked around the dim interior of the cave, studying it. She realized that this was Coblaith's lair, the place where she hid from the Ceardannan and the prying eyes of others during the daytime. It was the reason she was like a ghost, appearing and disappearing, fleeting when there was danger. When her lips could finally move, she smiled. "So, this is where you come when you go away," she said.

Coblaith's eyes were focused on the flames as if sucking the warmth through them. "We will remain here until they have stopped looking for us. Then, we will save the Clootie Well."

"What have we to eat?" Annie asked. As her body warmed her stomach was beginning to gurgle.

Coblaith rifled through a pile of items near the fire and produced some dried dandelions and mushrooms, offering Annie one of each. The taste was bitter, and she chewed them slowly. It would have to do until they could go out again and forage in the woods. She thought dismally of the sweet winter berries and the bags of salt and oats they had left behind in the catacomb under the castle. A warm bannock spread with berries would sure taste good. "Will we starve to death now?" she asked.

"No, not if we are smart," said the old woman. "Spring will be here soon, and we will have plenty again. The earth will provide."

Annie swallowed her meager supper and they both fell asleep, lulled by the warmth of the fire.

In the morning Annie jolted awake from the cold and immediately rekindled the fire. Coblaith was rolled up in her blanket, sound asleep and Annie studied the old face in the firelight. It was not an ugly face and somehow it seemed familiar now, as if she had known the old woman all her life.

148

She no longer cringed at her scoldings and lectures which were somehow less offensive than her Da's harsh words. They had bonded in a strange sort of way. Although Coblaith could sometimes spit words out like venom, she seemed to be a harmless old reptile.

When Coblaith finally opened her eyes and sat up, Annie could tell there was something on her mind.

"You must go fetch our food," she said simply. "We must make use of everything now and not waste it."

"Why *me*?" Annie was not looking forward to another freezing trek through the snow.

"You are younger and quicker than I am."

"But those men will be looking for us," replied Annie. "They will lock me up again!"

"You must wait until it is dark. Those men will not venture out in the night. They will all be huddled around their fires at home. No, you must go tonight."

"What if they destroyed everything like they did the Clootie Well? What will we eat then?"

"It is our only chance, Annie. You must go."

They spent the day sewing. Coblaith showed Annie how to piece bits of wool together to make their clothes warmer, to line their shoes to protect their frostbitten feet from the cold. By the end of the day Annie had a new pair of shoes for walking in the snow, lined on the inside now with soft fleece and on the outside with thick sheep hide. She put on her two dresses one over the other and her shawl, now padded with wool, and flung an empty sack over her shoulder before she ventured out into the snowy moonlight.

The meadow outside the castle walls had taken on a translucent blue color and the road was covered in snow and invisible to the naked eye. It was a land of silent fragility; Annie's footfalls were like whispers for the new powder was soft and pliant. She hurried along wanting her errand to be over so she could return to the warmth of the cave, across the slippery bridge, through the crumbling masonry of the gatehouse. When she reached the tower, she fumbled in her pocket for a flint with which to light the torch. Banging stick against the wall to break loose the icy crust that had formed in the night, she warmed it with her hands before she struck a flame to it. It took several attempts before a tiny flame began to flicker and she started down the stairs.

The first thing she noticed was that the grate had been flung open; the padlock with the key still inserted in it was lying on the floor. The men must have come back for them only to find they had escaped. The rest of the catacomb looked untouched, unmolested. She quickly found the corner where the bags of oats and salt were hidden and put them into her sack. Gathering up the tinder and kindling and the winter berries she turned to leave but something made her pause and approach the grate again. Putting down the sack, she got on her hands and knees and lowered the torch into the hole so she could see. The bats had returned to their suspended beds and ignored her; the tide from the loch had returned and the opening to the underground cave was once again submerged and hidden beneath the water. She thought of Coblaith's sea chest. *There might be something useful inside it*, she thought. *Might as well look while I am here* but then she quickly decided against it. The chest contained Coblaith's personal belongings. Something told her it would be rude to snoop through them without permission. The last thing she wanted to do was anger Coblaith again. Besides, lingering too long in the castle was dangerous; the men could return at any moment.

Outside the cold did not bother her; she was anxious to leave this place. She felt like she was flying over the snow on the back of an invisible destrier. The wind was behind her, pushing her on and the sack on her back seemed weightless. She reached the Clootie Well and the fallen tree, still covered with snow and silvery icicles, and took the path toward the rock cliffs. It was a bit difficult pulling the sack up behind her, but she managed to make it to the top, to the cave opening.

"Coblaith!" she called out.

The old woman still had not risen. She was still rolled up in her blanket next to the dwindling fire. Annie dropped the sack and sat down.

"Why have you let the fire grow cold? Must I do *everything* around here?"

She was not trying to be disrespectful. She was teasing Coblaith, imitating the old woman's usual abrasive style. Grinning, Annie reached out and gently jostled the woman's shoulder.

"Coblaith! Up with you now! We have work to do, bannocks to prepare, berries to crush! I brought the food and kindling for the fire. There is no time for sleeping!"

CHAPTER EIGHTEEN "BATTLE OF THE NOBLES"

Conachar mourned the loss of his son for many months and now spent most of his time in the catacomb beneath the castle. He would receive an occasional letter from William telling of the progress being made on the castle in Cromarty and he sometimes considered leaving Airchartdan and following him. His wise healer advised against it.

"He must be allowed to stand alone and make his own way," she told him. "He cannot do that if his father hovers over him all his life. Let him shine, Conachar. Let the great castle in Cromarty be his badge of honor."

So Conachar remained in Airchartdan. His disillusioned men began to scatter to the wind. Some went off to join the king's army. Others found employment in the little town of Drumnadrochit, their faith in their laird weakening with every month that passed. Past his prime now, Conachar's hair had turned grey, his muscles had grown soft, and his demeanor had become depressed and sullen. Even his healer could not bring him out of it. No spell she could cast could take away the loneliness he felt. He had lost his son and somehow he knew young William would not return from Cromarty. He knew from personal experience that it would take years to build a castle and, as she reminded him, he would not live forever.

Finally, on a warm spring day the inevitable happened. Conachar died cradled in her arms and the few of his men who remained buried his body in the courtyard, next to the grave mound of his ancestor Emchath. They placed a standing stone on his grave. The healer moved her things out of the catacomb that very day and returned to her cave in the woods, leaving

Airchartdan behind but secreting Conachar's sword beneath her clothing. When she reached the Clootie Well, she decided to bury it beneath the tree rather than hang it in plain sight for someone to steal. By the time of his burial, the rest of his men had fled; some, growing weary and bored, returned to Ireland. A few married their sweethearts from Drumnadrochit and settled there. For a time, Airchartdan was abandoned.

Not long after, William the Lion died too; it was not a brave death in battle but a slow passing in his bed of natural old age. His crown had quickly passed to his heirs, but the line of succession was soon broken with the deaths of his son, his grandson and granddaughter and, with no king on the throne, once again Scotland was plunged into civil war. There was bloodshed everywhere it seemed. After William's death his son Alexander, in a quandary over what to do with the old castle, had hastily granted ownership of it to his faithful manservant, Thomas De Lundin and the family moved in almost immediately. The healer watched from her vantage point deep in the woods as the courtyard filled with livestock and a new standard was hoisted on the flagpole above the grey battlements. Wagons began arriving almost daily, bringing more and more people until the place was as busy as a hive of bees. Every day there was a line of women doing laundry along the shore, men were plowing the grassy knoll to make room for crops and building fences to keep their sheep from wandering too far; the road to Drumnadrochit soon turned into a busy thoroughfare.

The nobles could not decide who had the stronger claim to the throne. Three clans among the others, the Balllols, the Bruces and the Comyns, stood out as the main contenders, but with no clear candidate in sight, they turned to King Edward I of England to intercede to help solve their dilemma. They trusted the English king guardedly mainly because they all held title to

English lands as well as their estates in Scotland and straddled the fence regarding their loyalty. Secretly they supported the English king in the south, sometimes fighting alongside Edward's troops against their own countrymen while supporting the clans in the north. Edward, however, had plans of his own. He immediately demanded they all declare homage to him as overlord. He then surprised them all by naming John Balliol, the weakest man he could have chosen from among them, to rule in his name and the most likely to bow to his wishes. It wasn't long before he demanded that Balliol abdicate and relinquish power to Edward himself. The people of Scotland exploded in revolt and King Edward went on the attack, taking Scottish castles one after another into his possession, including Airchartdan, and assigning various constables to hold them for England. The clans retaliated by attacking Airchartdan repeatedly to run the English out and dominion over the castle see-sawed back and forth. Finally, around the time King Edward installed Alexander Comyn as governor, the castle was given a new name: Urquhart Castle, *the castle by the woods.*

While the nobles continued to support both sides, the people were furious at what they deemed a betrayal, and Robert the Bruce finally decided it was time to stand against Edward. It happened one night after yet another scrimmage between the English and the Scots, as he sat down to eat his supper with several English soldiers with whom he had been fighting to protect his lands in England. They were all tired and filthy from the day's fighting, covered in blood and dirt and so exhausted they did not bother to wash themselves. As they broke bread together one of the soldiers remarked, "Look at the Bruce! He is eating his own blood!"

Bruce stopped eating and, rising abruptly, he left the table, rushing down to a nearby river to bathe. The awful reality of the matter had finally dawned on him. It was true! He *was* eating his own blood by shedding the blood of his fellow Scots! He was no better than the Baillols and the Comyns who were only puppets to the king of England. Guilt overtook him and he swore that night that he would never again betray his country.

Over the next few months, he began gathering a small group of patriotic Scots and went on a rampage across the lowlands to oust the English. When he could not convince John Comyn to join him in his rebellion, he murdered him on the altar of a church. He then rode north and marched through the Great Glen to recover all the Scottish castles under English control along the way. King Edward had recently executed the people's hero William Wallace but now they had someone new to fight for them and they soon flocked to the Bruce's side. He was crowned at Scone shortly after, although it would still be years before the wars ended and England would finally recognize him as the rightful king.

The Bruce suffered greatly by his decision to fight for Scotland. His brothers were killed, his wife and child were taken prisoner and he narrowly missed assassination several times. In addition, Bruce, a religious man, had been excommunicated by the Pope for committing murder on sacred ground. Even though he was the king, he found himself constantly on the run, hiding away in caves and obscure holdfasts and eventually escaping to Ireland, all the while gaining more support from his countrymen. When he returned from Ireland to save his wife and family, he was determined to mount a strong resistance against the English takeover.

By the time he sailed up Loch Ness and arrived at the castle by the woods it had been reduced to an empty shell. Having changed hands many times over the years as the Scots fought to keep the English out it had continued to be the sight of many raids and sieges between rival clans as well as attacks

155

from fanatical religious mobs. Although many attempts had been made to repair and rebuild it, now only the outer wall and a few structures remained intact. In the next few years that followed there were more attacks, thieves stripping it of furniture, weaponry, livestock and even the castle gates. After bombardments from deadly English cannons over the years its battlements were soon weakening and needed repair, and yet it stood like a proud highlander on the promontory overlooking Loch Ness, weathered and broken but still defiant and brave.

Robert the Bruce was determined to save it from ruin. He took time to have his men make repairs to the damaged walls. Before he moved on in his quest to rid the rest of Scotland of the English invaders he secured the castle, leaving a few trusted men behind to guard it in his absence. Although they had no way of knowing it then the castle by the woods would soon have the reputation of being the last castle in the highlands under Scottish control.

All that summer, the healer laid low, and the inhabitants of Urquhart Castle never knew she was watching them from afar. At first, she carried on her life under the cover of darkness and survived for months in silence and solitude. Lulled into a false sense of security, with Bruce's men standing guard on the battlements and treating the castle with respect, she began venturing further and further from her lair to pick berries and gather greens and mushrooms in the daylight hours. Fighting between the Bruce and King Edward had apparently moved on to the south and the unrest between the clans temporarily died down. It was a welcome period of peace and tranquility across the Great Glen.

One afternoon, as the gentle Druid drew water from the Clootie Well, she heard a great commotion coming from the road. The grunting and heavy breathing of dozens of horses and the rotations of noisy wooden wheels as they rolled over the rutted road, invaded the sanctuary beneath the trees. Sensing danger was near, she hurried back to the cave and huddled there with her ear to the stone walls. When the sounds grew even closer and became deafening, out into the sunny meadow wagonloads of cut lumber, huge coils of rope, piles of heavy stones and oak barrels pulled by teams of horses came rolling into view. Following the wagons rode hundreds of well-armed English soldiers on horseback.

Bruce's men on the battlements heard it too and they gathered to watch the English army, with King Edward himself in the vanguard, as the caravan stopped, and the men began to unload the wagons. They worked for hours, until the sun had set, and they rested for the night. The following day they were up with the dawn to continue their project in front of the castle. Archers were summoned to the walls and a barrage of arrows was loosed on the English soldiers, but to no avail; the English were too far away. They waited.

Edward's men continued to work and in two days' time they had assembled an enormous wheel, attached to heavy ropes and cables. In horror Bruce's men watched as a massive fire was lit; the stone balls were doused with oil and lighted. One by one the fiery missiles were flung at the walls; like a giant slingshot, they pounded away at the ancient palisade that had for centuries protected the castle. Flaming arrows were no longer the bane of Castle Urquhart. Now it was a battle of stone against stone. The walls could not withstand an attack of this magnitude and they began to crumble. When it was apparent they could not defend their position any longer, Bruce's men fled to the water and escaped across the loch by boat.

CHAPTER NINETEEN "ENEMIES ABOUND"

Annie and Coblaith managed to survive the winter in the cave by pure grit and determination. The Clootie Well provided them with water and the old woman taught the girl how to find all the edible plants in the forest. By the time their salt and oats ran out and they had harvested the last of the mushrooms and summer greens that were left, spring came in like a breath of fresh air, melting away what was frozen, ushering in new life in the forest. The meadow that surrounded the old castle turned green once again and was soon populated with herds of sheep and highland cattle, but the two fugitives remained hidden away from the sight of the shepherds. They were both thinner and the second-hand clothes Annie wore hung limply from her body. Her once rosy cheeks had grown pale and sunken.

They found another tree not far from the one the men had destroyed and rehung the trinkets and talismans on its branches. Annie overheard Coblaith whispering a blessing over each one as she placed it. Birds perched in the surrounding trees out of curiosity to watch them.

"We could sure make use of some of these things," Annie complained to Coblaith. "How long does it take to get a blessing anyway?"

"These were all put here to keep sickness and death away, to give comfort and peace when needed. Those needs never leave us until we are buried in the ground, Lassie."

"Shall I put one up for you, Coblaith? A wish for a long life, maybe?"

The old woman shook her head. "I have had a life full of blessings; I dinnae' need more."

Annie giggled. The woman lived in a cave and had just survived a brutal winter, existing only on what the forest could provide. How could that possibly be a *blessing*? "Dinnae' you ever wish for a more comfortable home? For a feather bed and windows?"

"What would I need windows for when I can just walk outside and breathe the air?" She paused and thought for a moment. "A feather bed to sleep in might be nice though."

In the time they had spent together Annie had learned much from the old woman. Survival skills aside, she had learned how the creatures of the world could live in harmony with each other, each providing what the other needed in kind. Whenever they caught a fish, Coblaith would bury the head to fertilize the ground. Whenever they unearthed a tuber, she would slice off the top and replant it for the next season. It gave Annie pause to think. *What had she herself contributed to the world?* she wondered. She had cared for her Da and her brothers for years; she had helped Deidre for a short time. Now they were all gone, and she had no one left to help except Coblaith and Coblaith required little.

They had finished hanging all the trinkets that they could salvage from the mud and puddles of melted snow and were heading back to the road when the far-off sound of people approaching caused them to duck behind the brambles, watching to see who was coming. It had been months since the last garrison of Jacobites had marched through. These sounds were coming from the north, however, from the direction of Inverness. These could be returning soldiers! Was the war over? Annie's heart skipped. Could it be Alex and

159

Angus coming for her? She peered through the thick foliage, squinting her eyes then to make a wish.

The voices got louder; they were only yards away down the road now. They were the low, tired voices of defeat however, not the jubilant voices of victory. Suddenly the men were directly in front of where they hid in the bushes: dozens of bedraggled, bloody men, limping and stumbling along the muddy road. Some were pulling a litter with an injured soldier wrapped in bandages. They were all as thin as scarecrows, their once-fresh kilts and shirts now soiled and torn, their white cockades, now withered and dirty, hanging from their bonnets.

Coblaith was the first to stand up and reveal herself. The sight of her startled the men in the lead. Annie watched as the old woman went forward and knelt beside the prostrate man on the makeshift litter. Unwinding the cloth wrapped around the man's head, she saw her tear a bit off and tuck it under her sleeve.

"There is water here if you are thirsty," she said, leading them away from the road to the Clootie Well, "and I am a healer. I can help you with this man. He won't make it much further being bounced around on the road."

The men followed her into the brush and gathered around the strange Druid lady with curiosity, accepting her offer of a drink gladly.

"Can you dig bullets out of flesh?" one man asked her. "That's what ails him, and we have no surgeons among us."

"Aye," replied Coblaith. "You must bring him to my cave where I have a fire and I can care for him properly."

Annie was shocked that Coblaith would open their cave to these men, that she would reveal the hiding place that had shielded them from execution for months. Could they trust them, these bedraggled Jacobites? Or would the soldiers turn them over to the magistrate in Drumnadrochit? And where would they put them all? The cave was barely large enough for the two of them.

"We havna' much food to offer. It has been a lean winter. And my cave is small. Only room for the wounded one."

"No matter," said the man who seemed to be in charge. "We're on our way back to our homes to check on our families. We cannae' stay too long in one spot. The English army will hang us if'n they catch us."

The men drank their fill from the spring and followed them back through the woods to the cave. Annie noticed that some of the younger soldiers were staring and smiling at her, and she felt the color rise in her cheeks. Many of them were not much older than she was. While romance and the opposite sex had not occurred often to her with survival constantly on her mind it pleased her. Her eyes searched through the men's faces for those of her brothers. She fell behind them to avoid their stares and watched Coblaith lead them to the rock wall. They had to use ropes to pull the litter up to reach the cave and they laid the man near the fire.

"This is a right-cozy place you ladies have here. Have you been here all winter?"

"Aye."

"Who are you hiding from? The English army?"

There had been talk of soldiers who brutalized Scottish women. He looked at Annie pitifully and hoped that was not the case here.

"My name is Captain Rainie. These are my men who fought with me at Culloden."

Coblaith was busy making the injured man comfortable near the fire.

"Where is Culloden? Is that near Inverness?" Annie wanted to know. Maybe these men knew of her brothers.

"Aye," replied the captain. "It is where the bloody battle took place." He sighed deeply and hung his head. "We lost many men. It was a slaughter."

Annie's chin dropped and she felt a tear fall. "My brother went off with the Jacobites to fight. He never came back."

"I'm sorry, Lassie. He's probably lyin' out there in the field, but if'n he is you kin be sure at least he ain't hurtin' no more."

After they had made the injured man comfortable, the soldier prepared to leave them.

"I'll be back for him as soon as I can," said Captain Rainie. "I thank ye for helpin' him. Be careful. There will be English soldiers passing by this way on their way to Fort Augustus. Stay out of sight and dinnae' let them find you."

"We will be fine," replied Coblaith. "Dinnae' worry about us."

Annie stoked the fire and watched as Coblaith began to treat the injured man. He was awake but his eyes were dull with pain, his face pale and drawn. He said nothing as the old woman removed the bloody bandage from his forehead. She wet a piece of cloth and dabbed it on his skin, slowly revealing his wound. "No bullet here," she whispered. "Only a scratch. It will heal if'n you have time to rest." Her attention was then drawn to his leg. Just below the knee she found a deeper injury, now coagulated and festering. She concocted a smelly balm from forest herbs and plants, setting it aside and heated her knife in the coals.

She turned to Annie. "Fetch me some more water. He will need a bath. From the looks of him we'll have crawlin' critters in our beds fer sure."

Annie did as she was told and took the water bucket before she climbed down through the rocks and headed for the spring. By now the sun was high overhead, filtering down through the upper branches as if through a sieve, pricking the dark woods with needlepoints of light. The great glen had come alive again; the songs of birds that had been silent for months now drifted among the leaves. She looked up and down the road before she stepped out into the open. Now they not only had the men from Drumnadrochit who wanted to burn them as witches to worry about; now they had to hide from the English army too! What would be next to make their lives miserable? Would their persecution never end?

She filled the bucket to the brim from the well; Coblaith would need lots of water to bathe his filthy body and remove the bullet. Lugging it back to the rocks she pondered just how she would manage to carry it up to the cave without spilling half of it. As usual, Coblaith had the answer. She was standing above her with her hands on her hips. She dropped a piece of rope to pull it upward. "It certainly took ye long enough! Did ye go all the way to the loch to fetch it?"

Annie tied the rope around the handle and Coblaith hoisted it up the rock wall. By the time Annie entered the cave, the woman had already begun washing the blood and dirt away from the soldier's leg and had moved closer to him. "This will hurt a bit but try not to move. We will get the bullet out and then wash the rest of you."

The man moaned and cried out as the hot knife entered his flesh. Annie couldn't bear to look; she turned her head away. Deeper and deeper, Coblaith dug until she finally popped the piece of metal out and a fresh river of blood flowed behind it. Immediately, she pressed down on the wound with the palm of her hand and held it there until the bleeding stopped. "There," she said. "Now you should feel better."

She bathed him, discreetly removing his clothes and handing them to Annie for laundering. "Take these and wash them thoroughly. When they are clean hang them where the wind will dry them, in a bit of sunlight if'n you can find one. Then gather some more tinder and kindling to keep the fire burning."
Annie twisted her face. *More work*. It was always more work for her. Would there ever be a time for her to wander about picking flowers or dipping her toes along the shores of the loch? A day for daydreaming? After being cooped up all winter in the cold with Coblaith she was longing for a carefree day in the sun.

"I am not asking for myself," said Coblaith, sensing the girl's dismay. "Dinnae' you want to save this poor boy's life? Wouldna' ye want the same for yer brothers?"

Annie rolled her eyes and nodded sheepishly. "Aye. I would want that."

She took the soiled clothing and climbed down from the cave but left the bucket behind before she sprinted out of the glen and down the bank to the rocky shore just beyond the old castle. Walking out into the bright sunshine brought a smile to her face. The breeze smelled of springtime, of heather and musk thistle. The water was still ice-cold, remnant of the recently melted snow, and her hands turned purple as she dipped them in to wash out the bloody garments. She squeezed and twisted until the water from the cloth rinsed clear and found a sunny rock on which to lay them and sat for a few indulgent moments letting the warmth linger on her face. Disregarding the chill of the wet sand, she pulled off her shoes and made footprints up the beach, gathering pieces of driftwood that had dried and withered brown grass for tinder from before the snow. Not far away stood the castle ruins, staring down at her with its narrow-windowed eyes from beneath its crenelled bonnet. She had loved the castle at first but now she wasn't sure how she felt about it. Nothing good had happened here. She had lost her entire family including the adopted family she had found in the Ceardannan. Now she was an exile from *everywhere* it seemed. She remembered her plan to go to Inverness alone, but wondered now if that was a good idea, what with the English army on the move and the men from the village who might still want her dead.

Returning to the rock, she turned the clothing over to let the sun dry it from the other side. She ran her fingers over the man's shirt, feeling the buttons and smoothing out the collar and it brought back memories of doing her brothers' laundry. Closing her eyes, she was transported to another day, to a peaceful world where the waves were gently caressing the shore and the breeze taking away the stuffiness and confinement of the cave. So much had happened in her short life and in such quick succession there had hardly been time to grieve the loss of her family. Now, she and Coblaith were accused of being witches and had been forced to hide away in a cold cave all winter. It hardly seemed real, and it was fathoms away from her life in Cromarty. She opened her eyes again to the stark reality of the present.

Her attention was drawn toward a lone eagle flying overhead, its wide, brown wings glistening brilliantly in the sun, its white tail flailing out behind it as it glided on the wind. She watched it as it lowered its mighty claws and came to perch on the battlement of the castle tower, proceeding to preen and groom itself all the while keeping an alert eye out for fish jumping in the loch. She watched it for a few moments in awe. Such a magnificent creature it was, so graceful and powerful! Suddenly it fluttered upward, as if startled by sound or movement and swooped out over the water and flew away. Absent-mindedly Annie glanced back at the tower where the bird had been and gasped when she saw him….an English soldier staring down at her! Her heart jumped and she leapt to her feet, grabbed the clothing from the rock and made a hasty dash for the cover of the trees. She was sure he had seen her! Panic set in as she frantically ran through the bushes and brambles, not really realizing what direction she was going, only desperately wanting to escape his eyes. Redcoats in the castle! Just like back in Cromarty!

She knew it would not be wise to return to the cave directly and possibly reveal their hiding place, just in case the soldier sent someone to follow her so when she reached the road, she crossed over it and ran north, deeper into the glen, out of sight. She hadn't time to listen for footsteps behind her. Now she was rushing through unfamiliar woods and strange rock formations, trying to put distance between herself and the English soldiers. Climbing over one large rock she discovered a small indentation below it, barely large enough for man or beast to fit but completely concealed from the path. She threw herself onto the ground and rolled into it, pulling her arms and legs inside and closing her eyes. She tried to slow her breathing and listen to the sounds in the surrounding woods.

Minutes passed and then she heard horses on the road and men talking nearby. *Much too near.* She had believed she was further away, that sounds carried among the trees, but the voices seemed only feet away, practically on top of her! She had never felt fear more acutely in her life, not even when they had been imprisoned in the castle. Tears trickled down her cheeks and she worried about Coblaith. Had she run far enough away from the cave to protect her?

Annie laid there for hours, not making a sound, until the sun began to set, evident from the shifting of light through the trees. Soon it would be dark. The voices and the horses seemed to have gone away and she contemplated climbing out while she could still see her surroundings. She gathered up the soldier's clothing and emerged, her ears still on alert for the sounds of her pursuers. There was nothing except the calling of the nightbirds and the chattering of squirrels in the branches above her.

She found her way back to the road and by the time she reached the path to the Clootie Well and knew where she was the darkness had fallen. She passed the water bucket she had left behind; someone had overturned it. That worried her. She hurried to the rock wall and began the climb up its stone face. Inside, there was no sign of a fire; the cave was as dark as pitch. Annie blindly inched her way along, trying to avoid stepping on the sleeping soldier. She felt his blanket with her foot and tiptoed softly around it.

"It's just me, Sir. No need to be afraid," she whispered.

When she reached the firepit her eyes had adjusted to the darkness. "Coblaith? Where are you? Are you asleep?"

There was no sound. Annie put down the laundry and searched for the flint to light the tinder. A small blue flame danced timidly out of the darkness. At that moment, she realized the soldier was gone; his bed was empty. Coblaith was gone too! In the fire's glow she could see a trail of blood across the floor, and she could only hope that it was from the soldier's wound. "Coblaith!" she called again. Again, there was no answer.

In horror she remembered the overturned bucket and realized by leaving it there in plain sight she must have led the English soldiers directly to the cave! How foolish Annie had been, languishing on the shore in the sun, disregarding the danger they were in, tempting fate. The soldiers must have discovered where Coblaith was hiding and taken both her and the Jacobite soldier prisoner. It was the only explanation. The man was incapable of walking on his own and Coblaith was not strong enough to carry him. There was only one thing to do! She had to go in search for Coblaith!

Without worrying about taking her belongings, she dashed out of the cave, climbing down to the ground frantically in the darkness. She ran up the road leaving the fear she had felt behind her. Just *how* she would manage a rescue, one girl against the English army, she had no idea, but she was determined to be imprisoned with Coblaith if needed. She had no weapon to defend herself. All she knew was that Coblaith was her friend and she needed to *try*.

When Annie reached the edge of the woods, she crouched down behind some brush and strained her eyes toward the castle, looking for signs of movement on the battlements, for activity around the gate, but saw none. There were no torches burning on the tower. Across the meadow there were no sounds except the occasional bleating of a faraway ewe calling to her lamb. In the air there was no hint of smoke from campfires. Annie stood up and took a deep breath, summoning all her courage and determination. If the English had taken Coblaith prisoner she knew where they would have her! She had to get inside the castle walls somehow, the English army be damned!

Somewhere in the darkness she heard a horse nicker. She took one step toward the road, ready to break into a run for the castle when a strong masculine arm came out of the darkness and grabbed her. He held her close and whispered, "Shhhhhhh." She could feel the hardness of his chest against her back, the warmth of his breath on her neck. She struggled frantically against him but hadn't the strength to pull herself away; her screams were muffled in the palm of his hand.

CHAPTER TWENTY "BLOODY TUG OF WAR"

The unrest continued across Scotland. After the battle between the English and Robert the Bruce's army at Bannockburn, a temporary truce took place and for a while King Edward, who was failing in health, pulled back his forces. But it wasn't long before the fighting began again. When the English king died, his son, Edward II, was even worse, wreaking as much destruction on Scotland as his father had. His armies ventured further north into the highlands once again, burning and looting and destroying every Scottish stronghold in their path. The clans had been forced to dismantle and they went underground, holding meetings in secret. The English king imposed new laws, claiming any support given to the Bruce to be acts of treason. The Bruce was growing old now. When he finally died in his bed, his son, David II, was only five years old and unable to tie his own shoes much less rule a country. For a while the prince's regents took control of Scotland until the boy was old enough to rule and clan warfare erupted again.

Urquhart Castle was still standing but much of it had been destroyed. After the last English attack with the deadly trebuchet, it had been left to ruin, only of value to those who wanted to plunder it to use in other projects. It became a ghost-castle, a quarry of broken stone, a graveyard of dead memories. Scotland was still at war with England. Loch Ness became a highway of English warships and frequent attacks. Although the castle has been reduced almost to rubble, its strategic location still made it valuable. The English stationed a garrison within its walls only to be attacked and driven off soon after by the MacDonald clan of the western isles who held the castle but did nothing to fortify it.

When James IV was crowned King of Scotland, he was dismayed by the ruinous condition of Urquhart Castle. He relieved the MacDonalds and granted possession of it to the nearby Grant clan under the condition that they rehabilitate it and build a strong tower on the promontory. Angered at being set aside, the MacDonalds returned in force and attacked again, stripping it of its ships and guns. England, meantime, had troubles of its own and had temporarily abandoned the site, leaving the highland clans to fight over it. In addition to the Clan Grant and Clan MacDonald, battles broke out among the religious factions in Scotland and soon the castle was being attacked by all sides. It became a status symbol, not much more than a placeholder and a show of vanity.

When King James was killed at the Battle of Flodden, the MacDonald clan once again claimed possession of the castle. They attacked in what became known as the Great Raid, in which they stole all the cattle and other livestock. They stripped it of all its furniture and weaponry, even the castle gates. When the Grants retaliated and regained control, a mob of Presbyterian Covenanters broke into the castle, running Lady Mary Grant out in the dead of night in her nightgown. They disliked the lady of the castle because she was an Episcopalian.

Castle Urquhart was losing favor. By now there was so little left of it, neither side thought it was worth fighting for, so it fell even further into ruin and was soon only being used as a source of building materials. When the English general Oliver Cromwell invaded Scotland, he disregarded the location entirely and built forts at either end of the Great Glen. When James VII was deposed after the Revolution of 1688, the Grants, who were now supporting the English, took control once again. They garrisoned the castle with two hundred soldiers until a group of Jacobites laid siege to it. Finally, the

Grants abandoned it again, blowing up the gatehouse before they fled to discourage any further use by the *anyone*.

CHAPTER TWENTY-ONE
"COBLAITH'S TREASURES"

Annie finally gave up her struggle in the darkness and the man who had her firmly wrapped in his arms finally spoke.

"Be still, Lassie. I mean you no harm. Dinnae' you remember me? Captain Rainie! I came back to check on the welfare of my soldier."

Annie wriggled out of the captain's grasp, and he released her. While she caught her breath, he continued, "When I found no one in the cave, I assumed he was either dead and buried or had recovered and was hiding with you ladies deeper in the woods."

Annie could not see his face, but she recognized his voice. It was a deep, comforting voice and reminded her of her brother Alex. "I dinnae' know where they are. The English spotted me doing laundry on the shore and followed me, so I had no choice but to hide. By the time I could return to the cave, they were gone. The English must have taken them prisoner."

Captain Rainie sighed deeply. "I was afraid that might happen. The English army has moved on now, toward Fort Augustus I would imagine. If they have taken them prisoner, that is where they will hold them."

Annie fell to her knees and began to cry. She was tired and weary of losing everything and everyone she cared about. Coblaith had become like a mother to her, like the mother she never had. The guilt she felt knowing that she had foolishly led the English soldiers back to the cave weighed over her like the yoke old Bobbin used to wear. Her nose burned, her chest ached, her tears flowed in rivulets down her chest. The captain sat down beside her and draped a comforting arm around her shoulders. "Don't cry, Lass. Let me get you out of here. I will take you to my sister's farm in the hills above Drumnadrochit. You will be safe there. You cannae' stay here all alone."

"I cannae' leave here!" she said sharply. "If'n my brother comes back, or they release Coblaith, and she goes a'lookin' fer me, I havta' be here where they kin find me!"

"I will go to Fort Augustus to see what I kin find out," he assured her. "Meanwhile, I have to get you to a safe place. I promise I will come back for you."

More promises, thought Annie sourly, *empty promises that no one ever keeps.* Alex, Deidre, the whole lot of them. Liars all! Why should she trust this Jacobite captain any more than she had trusted her own? She had to face it, that she was truly abandoned by everyone she knew, and it was time to start making her own decisions.

"I will not leave this place. I must stay with the castle."

"You *must* come with me! I cannae' leave you here all alone. There will surely be more English garrisons coming through. The war did not end with Culloden. They will not be satisfied until they have crushed the life out of all the Scots. Of that you kin be sure. Let me at least help you. My sister is a good woman. She will take care of you. You will be out of danger there."

Annie was silent for several long moments before she spoke again. Now her words were more determined. She was not a child who could be ordered about. She had to be strong and make her own decisions. "I will come with you to Fort Augustus to find Coblaith and then I will return here to the castle."

"That would not be wise, Lassie! Even with me at your side, the roads are not safe!"

"I will go with you to Fort Augustus or nowhere at all," she said plainly.

The captain was willing to help, even if he thought the plan was a dangerous one. "Very well. I suppose I'd rather have you with me than staying in that abandoned castle all alone. Gather up your belongings and we'll leave at first light."

Annie climbed back up the rock wall and packed everything she owned into her old knapsack. Dawn was beginning to filter through the trees, reflecting on the emptiness within the cold stones. The captain was waiting for her below and she paused at the opening to the cave to stare at him. He looked somehow different than the man she had first met that day on the road. No longer dressed in his kilt and Jacobite bonnet, he had changed to rough-hide breeches and a loose home-spun shirt; a stocking cap was pulled down over his ears. His face was handsome, his physique was lean and well-muscled.

"I need to go back to the dungeon in the castle. Coblaith will need her things too."

He hoisted her bag onto his horse's back and walked with her across the meadow and through the gatehouse. He tied up the horse on the bridge and they made their way on foot across the courtyard, following the path Annie knew so well. Down the spiral stair, she led the way, her hands resting on the familiar stones to guide them as they went. She stared into the shadows thinking of her dear friend. *Poor Coblaith!* How she hoped the old woman was not suffering at the hands of the English soldiers! She could almost imagine her wrinkled old face staring back at her. She could hear her gravelly voice, telling her to get up and get to work before the day was nigh. The sound of the water moving beneath the stone floor

175

reminded her of her mission. She found a flint near the firepit and scratching it against the rock wall, she lit a torch and handed it to the captain before she knelt and stared into the hole. She let herself down slowly, remembering how roughly the men from Drumnadrochit had treated them, throwing them down onto the hard stone; the purple bruises it had left on her body remained for weeks. He jumped down and followed her, as she led him along the damp ledge toward Coblaith's old sea chest. While he held the torch above her, she noticed it for the first time in direct light. The box was warped and rusted from the damp air; its hinges creaked hideously as she lifted the lid. From its interior it emitted the pungent smell of mildew. She began digging through the contents. How long had it been here, rotting away in the cave? Months? Years? Centuries?

She found the metal box that had contained the half-pennies before and opened it only to be disappointed to find it empty; she pulled out the strange piece of forked wood that Coblaith used in her water rituals which Annie did not yet understand and tucked it under her arm. There were other trinkets too, necklaces made from nuts and seeds, the skeletons of rodents, dried and preserved, things she had never seen before.

"We cannae' take all this rubbish," said the captain. "I only have one horse and he will be carryin' two on his back."

Annie nodded. "I am only looking for what she might need to escape. She has magical things she uses to…."

She stopped in mid-sentence. The captain was staring at her with suspicion in his eyes. Annie could tell what he was thinking. "She is not a witch, if that is what you fear. She is a Druid, and she has powers neither you nor I have but she is a good woman, I assure you."

"Well, that could still get her hanged or burned alive," he replied, shaking his head sadly. "I hope this isna' all for nothing."

Annie reached up and adjusted the torch in the captain's hand to shine the light deeper into the recesses of the chest. There in a corner, was another small box made of wood with a silver clasp. She flipped it open with her fingers.

"What is it?" he asked.

Annie was speechless. She shook her head without uttering a word. There in the wooden box was a collection of buttons, a needle, and a spool of thread. He peered over her shoulder, curious to see the reason for the look of surprise on her face.

"It's just a box of bawbees," he said flatly.

"What is a bawbee?"

The captain tilted his head. "I dunno exactly. Old Gaelic legend says the kelpie in the loch leaves them in exchange every time he…."

Annie felt a long cold chill creep up her spine. "Every time he *what*?"

"It's nothing. Just an old legend. Been around for hundreds of years. Faerie tales to keep children from playing in the loch, I expect."

She turned around and gripped his shoulder tightly. "In exchange for *what*, Captain?"

"In exchange for lives he has taken."

She returned the box in horror and began to dig frantically deeper into the chest. Something compelled her, a strange feeling had come over her; she had no idea why. She could hear murmuring coming from the walls, low and monotone, like the faraway buzzing of a hive of bees. She had no idea what she was looking for but when she found it it took her breath away and she had to steady herself with one hand against the stone wall in disbelief.

In the very bottom of the chest, she touched something made of wool. It had fringed edges and many holes in it chewed by hungry moths. When Annie drew it out and held it up to the light, she could see it was a plaid tartan. She blinked and refocused her eyes in the darkness thinking they were fooling her. She examined it closely. No, there was no mistaking the pattern in the cloth; it was the same purple and green fabric she knew so well, the very fabric that had cradled her head and soaked up her tears for most of her life. How had Coblaith ever come into possession of the *Urquhart family tartan*? She pulled it from the chest and buried her nose in it. It had a different smell than her mother's tartan, but it was cut from the same cloth; of *that* she was sure. Her mind was confused, swimming in a murky pool.

The captain caught her in his arms just as she began to collapse in shock. His eyes widened when he saw what she held in her hands. "We cannae' take that along! Since Culloden the English king has forbidden the clans to display their colors in public. If'n we cross paths with soldiers our own lives would be in danger. No, you must leave that tartan behind."

Annie reluctantly replaced it into the chest, letting her hand rest on it for a moment. She could not explain her epiphany to him. It hardly made sense in her own mind.

The tartan, the buttons, the cryptic hints from Coblaith about *who* Annie was. She remembered the old woman's accusatory words: *you stole from your descendants, YOU of all people!*

How did she seem to know all about her family? Who was Coblaith? More importantly, who was Annie Urquhart?

CHAPTER TWENTY-TWO
"ASHES TO ASHES"

Before they set out on the road to Fort Augustus, Captain Rainey insisted they ride up the hill to Drumnadrochit to purchase food for their journey. There was no telling how long it would take them to find Coblaith and the soldier and they would probably have to camp in the woods for their safety. He installed Annie securely on his saddle and walked alongside the horse to lighten its load. It was a strange feeling for Annie to be riding a horse for the very first time in her life. Her legs barely reached the stirrups that were clearly fashioned for a male rider. Her short thighs were stretched to their limits to straddle the animal's back. Her knuckles were white where she gripped the leather tree. It wasn't the horse that scared her. Her nerves were still reeling from the discoveries in Coblaith's sea chest. What did it all mean? There were pieces of the puzzle that were missing. She had a lot of questions for her friend, if she ever saw her again.

"You *are* a wee thing," he said. "Just let your feet swing free. I've got him in hand. He willna' run away with you, I promise."

"I am not afraid. I have always loved horses. Why would I fear something I love?"

"You are a brave girl. I'll give ya that. Most girls would not be able to go through what you have and not faint dead away. I have seen soldiers on the battlefield who were not as brave as you are."

Annie smiled weakly. He was a nice man. A proper gentleman. Where would she be if he hadna' come back for her? She should be grateful and polite. Still, she was angry. Angry at the English army for kidnapping Coblaith when she had broken no law. Angry at her family and the Ceardannan for deserting her in such a place. She remembered painfully the rude merchant who had looked down at her as if Annie was something she had scraped off her shoe. She couldn't be seen in Drumnadrochit! She might pass one of those men on the street and be recognized!

"Stop!"

The captain halted the horse and looked up into Annie's eyes. "Is there something wrong? Are you feeling ill?"

"No. It's just that I cannae' go into the town with you. They think Coblaith and I were witches! They wanted to burn us alive!"

The captain scratched his head. "Very well, then," he replied. "There is a bridge over the river just outside of town. I can leave you there where you will be safe until I come back for ya".

Annie was glad to dismount from the horse's back; her legs were beginning to ache. She settled herself at the base of the bridge, close to the gurgling water, and laid her head on her knapsack. It was still early morn and everything around her was covered with dew, glistening in the first rays of the sun. The frogs were awake and vocal. In the planks above her head were several bird nests with squawking hatchlings and wary mothers who were eyeing her with suspicion. She opened her bag and retrieved the small box of what the captain called *bawbees*, wishing he would have allowed her to bring the tartan. It would have been a comfort in the dangerous world in which she found herself. She began to daydream of Cromarty and the Sutors and the bonnie blue firth of her youth. Would she ever see her hometown again? Would they be able to rescue Coblaith from the English soldiers? The captain came to her mind, the kind man who had taken it upon himself to protect her. Now he was in Drumnadrochit purchasing food to feed her and he wasn't even family! Annie knew there must be a benevolent god somewhere who was looking out for her, who had sent her an angel disguised as a Jacobite. And, yet she knew next to nothing about him. Where he came from. If he had family other than a sister in the highlands. Was he married? Did he have children? He was very young and handsome and romantic notions began to stir in her head.

But, what if he *didna'* return for her? The thought shot through her brain like a hot knife. She stood up, almost bumping her head on the low-lying planks and stretched her neck out, looking for him coming down the road. What if he had deserted her too? What if he decided she was becoming a burden and he never returned? She slumped back down in her hiding place, close to tears and began to make plans in her head, desperate plans, alternate plans. Her mind was spinning. She could return to the castle; she could gather food from the woods just like she had done the many months she had spent with Coblaith. She was a *survivor,* and she could *survive!* She felt the old familiar anger rising inside her. This was becoming an irritating pattern, the story of her life. Desertion, betrayal, indifference. It was almost unbearable.

A horse's hoof beats on the bridge broke her reverie.

"Dinnae' worry, Lassie. It is only me," called out a familiar voice.

Annie popped her head out again, feeling instantly guilty for doubting the kind captain. She hoisted her bag over her shoulder and climbed up to the road to meet him.

"I just realized," said the captain. "I dinnae' even know your Christian name. If'n we are to be travelling companions I suppose we should be properly introduced."

"I am very glad to meet you," she said. "I am Annie Urquhart."

He smiled and nodded. "Just like the castle."

Annie's face was blank with confusion. "The castle?"

"It explains why you were so reluctant to leave it."

"I dinnae' know what you mean, Sir. I was travelling through with the Ceardannan when we came across the ruins from the storm. I had never seen it before. That place has only brought sorrow and misery down on my head. I would have left it long ago if'n it hadna' been for Coblaith."

"But the castle carries your family name! Surely you knew that! It has been called Urquhart Castle for many years."

Annie was speechless. They had *another* family castle? One her Da had not told her about? Wasn't it bad enough that her ancestors had lost the old castle in Cromarty to bad debts and brought shame upon themselves that lasted generations? Now they had fallen so low they were plundering their own homes? What a fine family of ner-do-wells she had been born into!

"I knew nothing of this," she said. "I didna' know the castle even *had* a name."

She thought about it as she jumped up on the back of the captain's horse and could not extricate her mind from it for many miles as they rode along the road to Fort Augustus. He told her all that he knew about the history of the place. About Emchath and Conachar and the legend of the boar. She listened quietly, taking in all the stories. By the time they reached the deep woods, she had closed her eyes, her head leaning against the captain's muscular shoulders. When the horse stopped, he twisted his head to speak to her.

"You awake, Lassie?"

Annie blinked her eyes. The sun had passed over them and it was late afternoon. The loch had narrowed and ended at a tip of land that reached out over the water like a finger. Beneath the trees, the captain reined in the horse and threw his leg up over its neck to dismount. He reached up to take her bag and help her down.

"We'll camp here for the night," he told her as he tied the horse to the low-hanging branch of a tree. "I'll gather up some firewood to cook our supper."

He had purchased a portion of mutton, some potatoes and a loaf of bread in Drumnadrochit and had a small soapstone pot in his own bag which he unpacked and handed to her. Tied to the saddle tree was another small parcel wrapped in tissue paper. He gave it to her as well. "I thought you could use this."

Annie took the bundle and unwrapped the paper. In it she found a bolt of homespun cloth.

"It looks as though you havna' had new clothes in a while. I thought you could make yourself a new dress."

Annie had not felt so happy in a long time. She had never had a dress of her very own. For years she had worn her mother's castoffs and then inherited Deidre's faded old skirt; she had never experienced the luxury of having her very own *new* clothes. She didn't know what to say. Gifts seldom came her way.

"Thank ye," she mumbled, stroking the pristine cloth. "I am not very good at sewing. I mostly darned my brothers' socks and put buttons back on….and Coblaith taught me a bit."

Her brother's face flashed through her mind, and she recalled the day she had replaced the buttons on his shirt. "Do ya really

184

believe that story you told me about the kelpie and the....
what did you call them...the *bawbees*?"

"Naw. It was just a story. I've travelled the highlands all my life
and I havna' ever seen a kelpie."

"The reason I asked is because, when my brother disappeared,
I found the buttons from his shirt on the beach near the old
castle. It was so odd that he left us without a word. I hope you
are right and that it is just a faerie story."

The captain smiled. "I'm sure that is all it is, Lassie."

While she was not an accomplished seamstress, Annie *was* a
confident cook, and she quickly made a fire ring with stones. It
was the one talent in which she took pride. Uneducated and
unable to read or write, as her Da had never thought school
was necessary for girls, she had contented herself as a child
with listening to Alex as he read books to her. But food she
could handle quite well and before too long she had a mutton
stew simmering over the fire. Using hunks of the bread for
dipping, the two vagabonds consumed their supper
ravenously, scraping the bottom of the pot for the very last
morsels.

 "That was very good," said the captain. "You will make
someone a good wife someday."

She blushed and turned her head away as she took the pot
down to the water to wash it. When she returned the captain
had rekindled the fire and spread their blankets out on
opposite sides of the flames. He made himself comfortable on
the windward side and gave her the more sheltered spot
against a hollow log.

"Good night, Lassie," he said in a gentle voice.

"Good night, Captain."

185

When morning came, he was awake long before Annie, saddling his horse and filling his wineskin with water from the loch. He was ready to depart, when she finally opened her eyes.

"Oh, my! I didna' mean to oversleep. I havna' been so full in such a long time supper was like a lullaby to my belly."

The captain laughed. "I think ya will be safe here. It's not visible from the road. If'n you hear horses or soldiers, you must hide in the trees. I will be back…"

She looked at him incredulously. "You are not leaving me here! I am going with you to find Coblaith! That was our agreement!" She began gathering up her possessions and stuffing them into her knapsack.

"I dunno, Lassie. That might not be wise. I can go into town and see how things stand. If'n I have to escape I kin ride faster without ya."

Annie turned toward him. Her eyes locked with his and her nostrils flared. "No. I am gwine' with ya. I am gwine' to find Coblaith or at least what happened to her." She walked toward his horse and planted her feet firmly in the soil. "Yer not leavin' without me."

"You are by far the most stubborn lass I have ever met," he said smiling, stretching out his arm and hoisting her up behind the saddle. "I pity the English soldier who stands in your way!"

They rode out under a grey sky into the misty morning air and the horse plodded along a rutted road into town, crossing over a bridge and through an estuary of tall reeds and cattails. The road narrowed and soon became a bog. Once again, the captain dismounted and led their mount to lighten the load as the poor animal struggled to walk in the deep mud. Annie, sitting high in the saddle, could see above the green stalks and she spotted a stone building very near the shore of the loch. She pointed it out to the captain. "Look there, Captain! Is that the prison?"

Captain Rainey stood on tiptoe and arched his neck; he saw it too. "That appears to be a house of worship. See the colored windows? Prison windows have only iron bars."

They came to a fork in the road and followed the one that led in that direction until they came to the building in question: a small abbey. At the door, a man in a long, belted robe came out and greeted them. "Welcome, my children. Have ye come far? Come in, rest yourselves and have some refreshment."

"Thank ye, Sir but we are on an urgent mission. We are searching for friends who might have been taken as prisoner by the English. Can you tell us, are the streets in Fort Augustus safe to travel?"

The abbot lowered his head. "Ahhhh…. the streets are safe *now* after the battle and the great fire. We have had a short time of peace. But I am sure the English will return so ye should make your inquiries quickly and make haste from here."

The captain helped Annie down from the saddle, turning to the clergyman for more information. "*What* battle? *What* fire? We have just come from the north and have not heard any news."

"It would seem you are not the first to be seeking out the prison. A mob of Jacobites came through day before yesterday. Fought the English and laid siege to the prison and set the place afire. Folks tell me the English soldiers escaped in the night."

Annie could not contain herself. "And what of the *prisoners*? Did the English take them as well?"

"No, my dear. They took the horses and fled south. The prison was burned to the ground. There is still smoke in the air." He pointed toward the sky.

Captain Rainey and Annie stared at each other in horror. The captain put one foot in the stirrup and pulled himself back up into the saddle. He reached out for Annie. "Thank ye for the information. We must hurry and find out what has become of the prisoners."

"Should you not leave the lass here where it is safe? I will gladly watch over her."

It was Annie who answered him. "I think not, Sir. I am not afraid."

The captain laughed. "You may take her at her word. The English soldiers are no match for this girl when she makes up her mind."

They cantered off down the road toward the town. Annie strained to see over the captain's shoulder. She was the first one to spot the smoke rising in lazy spirals from the carcass of smoldering stone and wood that had once been the prison. Within minutes they were at the prison gate which had been demolished. The people of the town were wandering in the courtyard, digging through the rubble, salvaging what they could from the disaster. Annie jumped down from the horse's back and touched the shoulder of an old woman who looked like Coblaith from the back. The woman turned toward her.

"What have they done with the prisoners?" Annie asked frantically. "Were they released? Did the Jacobites save them?"

Shaking her head, the old woman turned back to rummaging through the ashes. "Whoever was left died with the castle, I am afraid. Did you have family in there, Lassie? I'm so sorry."

Without answering her, Annie rushed ahead, beneath the gatehouse, through the ash and burned wood, toward the main structure that was still belching smoke from its doors and windows. The captain was at her heels.

"Annie," he begged. "You cannae' go in there! It's not safe! The roof could collapse on you. It is still smoldering. You could burn yourself."

"I have to find her, Captain, and your man too. I have to know what happened to Coblaith, if she is alive or dead."

The interior of the prison was so full of smoke it was impossible to see more than a few feet in front of them. Annie pulled up her apron and covered her mouth and nose; the captain masked his face with the sleeve of his shirt. They ran through the rooms until they came across a row of cells, their locks still in place, some with the blackened dead fingers of corpses outstretched from beneath the door jambs.

"Coblaith!" Annie called out. "Coblaith are you here? We have come to get you out! Coblaith!"

There was no reply. The voices of the prisoners had all been silenced, their last breaths stifled by the smoke and flames.

The captain reached out and took her hand. "Come, Annie, we must get out of here or die from the smoke ourselves. I think it is safe to say no one in here is still alive."

"No….no….no…"

He pulled her to him, cradling her in his arms gently but firmly. He stroked her hair and felt her collapse against him. "Come

189

now, Annie. You must let it go…. you must let *her* go. We did our best. It is *over*."

CHAPTER TWENTY-THREE
"WHERE IS HOME?"

Annie awoke and brushed a strand of hair from her face. She looked around at the campsite where she had been sleeping and an open fire that was blazing, recognizing a familiar face across the flames.

"Good morning, Lassie."

For a few moments she thought it had all been a dream. A terrible dream. The prison, the fire, the blackened fingers of the people who had been burned to death. The expression on the captain's face quickly disillusioned her of that notion. She sat up and looked down at her apron, now covered in ash, and ran her fingers through her tangled hair.

"How did I get here? How long have I been sleeping?"

"Oh, quite a long time."

"I dinnae' remember." She looked over at the captain's horse grazing beneath the trees. "Did we ride here?"

"At least part of the way, you did. When I caught up with you, I believe your intention was to march all the way back to Urquhart Castle."

He handed her a roasted fish skewered on a branch.

"You must be hungry by now. I went fishing while you slept."

She was ravenous. Taking the fish she sank her teeth into it, devouring it quickly and drinking from the wineskin until she had drained it. Her memory ended back at the prison. She remembered nothing else, not the ride on horseback, not making camp, nothing.

"I'm sorry if I said anything rude to you, Captain. I was clearly not thinking clearly. I was just so….so…."

She broke down and began to cry, her tears streaming through the ash on her face.

"There, Lassie. You have done enough crying for a while. Why don't you go down to the water and wash your face? Then we can talk about where you want to go."

Annie retrieved a comb from her bag and walked slowly down to the loch. When she bent over the water and saw her reflection she was suddenly taken back in time. The memories of her dead mother sitting at the spinning wheel, of watching Alex march away with the Jacobites, of the burned-out prison that was Coblaith's grave. She stared at herself, at her cheeks that were streaked with black, at her hair that resembled a bird's nest on top of her head. She looked almost comical; her face was that of a court jester. Someone to make the children laugh. Why could she not remember laughing as a child? Why did her childhood seem so distant and so long ago? And, yet she was maturing; she was reminded of that fact every month. Her breasts were beginning to swell; her hips were widening as her body molded itself into the curves of a woman. Still, she felt like a child. Like a child who had never actually *been* a child. Her life seemed so short and yet long and full of sorrow. How desperately she wanted to return and be a little girl again, to be able to feel a mother's arms around her, to feel protected by her brother.

She splashed the cold water across her face, and it seemed to clear her head. How tiresome her moods must have become to Captain Rainey. She knew she mustn't alienate the only friend she had in the world. She ran the comb through her hair and dried her face in the folds of her apron until her appearance was respectable and returned to the campsite.

"Feel better now?" asked the captain.

"Aye," she replied sheepishly.

"Well, where is it we are going now? Castle Urquhart, I presume."

Annie hesitated. Where *did* she want to go? The castle had murdered everyone she loved. Perhaps the Ceardannan was right.... maybe it *was* cursed after all. Maybe *she* was cursed.

"I am sorry to be such a burden, Captain. I apologize for all that I have put you through. You have been so kind and generous to me; I wish I could repay you."

The captain frowned. "You owe me nothing. I came along with you because I wanted to."

"I am sure you have more important things to do, Sir."

"Actually, I dinnae' have anything more important than seeing that you get where you are going safely. Are you still of a mind to find your brothers in Inverness?"

Annie had to think about that. Was she being foolish? After the battle at Culloden the chances of finding Alex alive was doubtful and she had no idea where to look for Angus. She felt tears clouding her eyes again.

"There will be no more of that," said the captain, standing and gathering their belongings. "As a matter of fact, I am going to stay by your side until I see that beautiful smile again."

"Sir, I cannot delay you any longer from your affairs. You may leave me here. I am quite capable of finding my way back to the castle."

"And, what then, Lassie? Do you plan to live in those ruins all by yourself? What will you do when the English soldiers come

193

riding through again? Do you realize what could happen to you if they found you?"

"Aye."

"No, I will escort you wherever you wish to go."

She watched him as he saddled the horse and tamped out the fire. With all the horrible things that had happened to her, she had certainly been fortunate to have found such a friend.

"You must have family somewhere who are wondering where you are."

The captain shook his head. "I have no one except my married sister and I sent a letter to her when we were in Drumnadrochit to tell her where I was going. She'll not worry aboot me."

Annie could not think of a reply. She gathered her own things and together they mounted the horse. They rode along in silence. The clouds had come in from the north and the sky was grey above their heads, but she could feel the gloominess in her heart slowly fading.

"I believe we might have rain coming," said the captain. "Hold on tight and we will try to beat it."

She put her arms around him as he urged the horse into a canter, and they hurried back toward the castle. Annie closed her eyes and took comfort in the warmth of the captain's body.

 They reached the castle at dusk just ahead of the rain. While the captain tended to the horse in the courtyard, Annie went below to the catacomb and built a fire to take away the chill. She spread out their blankets on the stone floor and plumped their knapsacks into pillows for their weary heads. Supper would be a meager one; they had only a small piece of bread and one potato left. She went to Coblaith's old trunk to see if there were dried herbs she could use to make a soup of some kind.

The bats were restless, stretching and flapping their wings. Annie had noticed the waning moon earlier when the night sky had darkened enough to see its silhouette. Soon they would be flying outside to enjoy a few hours of freedom. She struck a flint and lit a torch, looking up at them, at the black creatures she had once been afraid of before she began searching through Coblaith's possessions. Now the old castle and its occupants had become as familiar to her as family. She found some herbs and mushrooms and a few nettles to add to the potato. It wouldn't be as filling as the mutton stew, but it would fill their empty stomachs until she could go into the woods to gather more ingredients. Returning to the fire she started their supper.

"I've never had nettle soup before," said the captain when he joined her. "I should have planned better. My horse is favoring his front leg a bit and I need to go to Drumnadrochit tomorrow to get some liniment. We may have to let him rest a day or two. I will visit the butcher while I am there and buy some meat and vegetables."

"Coblaith taught me how to make a meal out of practically nothing," said Annie. "It's not the king's banquet table but at least our stomachs willna' be gurgling all night long."

"You are a very handy woman to have around."

They drank their soup and ate their bread in silence in the firelight.

"And have you decided where it is you wish to go from here? You certainly cannae' stay here permanently."

Annie shrugged. She wasn't exactly sure herself. The castle felt comfortable, but she realized it was only a matter of time before another garrison of English soldiers marched through the glen and they would be in danger.

"I will think about that while you are in town tomorrow," she said, "after you have tended to your horse."

"I might be able to find work in Inverness without too much trouble. What little money I have saved willna' last too much longer."

CHAPTER TWENTY-FOUR "THE ADVENTURE CONTINUES"

In the morning, the captain quietly stoked the fire and covered a sleeping Annie with his own blanket before he hiked off to Drumnadrochit. By the time she opened her eyes she was tempted to close them again and go back to sleep. She smiled when she felt the extra blanket spread over her. Even Coblaith had never doted on her in such a thoughtful way. It was almost as if he had his arms around her, keeping her warm. Her mother's tartan had made her feel like that, sheltered and safe. But she needed to go into the woods and collect food, and she threw off her covering and braved the chill in the catacomb to get started.

Coblaith's sea chest hadn't much else that was of use to her; most of the junk that remained were things Annie didn't even recognize, odd things the old woman used in her rituals. She would have liked to have kept the chest, but she knew it was too bulky to carry on the horse, especially now that it was lame. She retrieved the strange, forked tool. She found a pair of rusty old scissors that would be helpful for her dressmaking and took them back to the fire where she sharpened them and rubbed away the rust. She pulled the bolt of cloth from her knapsack and began to work.

There was enough material for a simple dress and a little extra besides but without a pattern Annie had to make do on her own imagination. She stood up and removed Deidre's dress and used it instead. Annie doubled the cloth and placed the old worn dress upon it, weighting it down with stones. When she had cut out what looked something like a dress, she pulled the needle and thread from the box with the buttons, or *bawbees*, as the captain called them. The memory of Angus flashed through her mind. She had saved the buttons from his shirt she had found on the beach; they were still tucked away in her knapsack. As she threaded the needle her mind wandered to other ideas, things she could do to make their journey easier. She still did not know where they were going. Inverness? Cromarty? The road ahead was blurred. Even though her heart had been broken many times before, she was beginning to trust the captain.

When the dress was laid out ready to stitch, she turned to the remnants of material and stared at the piece that was left, trying to think of what she could make of it. It was square; if she folded it in half, it was the size of a bed pillow. How long had it been since she had the luxury of softness beneath her head? Not since she had her mother's tartan, and it was somewhere on a battlefield with Alex's body now. Probably bloody and torn. She was disappointed that the captain had been so adamant that they could not be discovered with a clan tartan in their possession but all at once she had an idea.

Returning to Coblaith's chest she retrieved the Urquhart family tartan. She rolled it up the size of a pillow and sewed the cloth around it. It was a perfect fit! She hugged its softness close to her and breathed in its scent. It did not conjure up memories of her mother. It smelled more like the dank catacomb, of the stone walls that had become her home. Strangely, it still comforted her somehow.

Annie's mind was darting from one idea to the next. She looked down at the box of buttons and threaded the needle again, this time making a double-stranded rope. She took out the buttons, one by one, and began stringing them together, finishing with the ones from Angus's shirt. When all the buttons had been strung, she knotted the thread and pulled it tight with her teeth. She slipped Deidre's dress back over her old dress and tied her shawl around her head. She gathered her apron to use as a bag and, placing the buttons, the scissors and the forked tool in it, dashed up the stairwell into the courtyard.

The captain's horse was lying on the hill where the old gravestones had been. Annie looked down at him sympathetically. The animal labored to stand up and began grazing on the grass. Annie reached out and rubbed his forehead. With the scissors, she snipped a bit of his forelock and tucked it into the bag.

By the time she reached the woods and the Clootie Well, things were becoming clearer to her, her future, her family legacy, her destiny. Annie first strung the bawbees on the tree between two low-hanging branches. Above them, in the crook between the trunk and the limbs, she anchored the wooden fork securely. Then she took the horsehair she had plucked from the captain's horse and knotted it tightly around a tiny sucker sprout. She closed her eyes and repeated a blessing she had heard Coblaith say. Then she stood back and smiled. At that moment, a ray of sunshine pierced the shade above her, and, like candles on a Christmas tree, danced on the leaves that were still sparkling from the morning dew.

She foraged for a long time, stuffing everything that was edible into her bag. When a couple of hours had passed, she headed back to the castle, stopping for a good long drink from the Clootie Well. The captain had returned before her and had wrapped the horse's leg with salt and rags. When she reached the catacomb, he already had mutton on the boil with potatoes and carrots. The aroma was heavenly to Annie's hungry nostrils.

"My that smells ever so good."

"Well," replied the captain, "I'm sure it's not as tasty as you will make it."

Annie smiled at him. "Aye, I have herbs from the woods to give it some flavor. Mutton tends to taste like wet wool without a little help."

The captain looked downtrodden.

"Oh, I didna' mean to say you had done anything wrong! A man wouldna' know such things about cooking any more than I know aboot fighting in a battle."

"You are probably right. I know nothing about cooking. When I am travelling, I usually chew on dried meat and raw vegetables. I miss my sister's cooking. What you have prepared for me the last few days reminds me of home."

"Where exactly *is* your home, Captain?"

"Here and there, I suppose. Since Culloden and my men disbanding, I have been drifting a bit. Before that I did a bit of farming work. My parents had a piece of land in Aberdeenshire, before they died."

"But the rest of your family. Surely you have other relatives somewhere. Someone you wish to visit?"

He shook his head sadly. "No, my sister is the only family I have left and I dinnae' visit her too often."

The quizzical expression on Annie's face prompted him to go on. She could not imagine anyone not wanting to visit family if they had the chance. She would have given anything to see hers again.

"My brother-in-law is not a Jacobite supporter. He strongly disapproves with my political beliefs."

"Oh," she replied. "I see."

But she *didn't* see. The world had become so complicated and fractured by the never-ending wars. Clans fought with other clans. The English fought with the Scots. Families broke apart because of their religious beliefs. Why couldna' they just all get along and love each other? "Sometimes I dinnae' understand the world we live in. Nothing stays the same. Nothing seems to last."

The captain agreed. He stared at her across the fire. "I see you have been busy sewing today."

"The dress isna' finished yet. My fingers were getting a bit sore. But I stitched together a pillow. See?"

"Aye, that's a fine pillow. I imagine sleeping on this hard stone night after night must be uncomfortable. A lady should have a nice soft place to lay her head."

Annie stirred the stew. Was that what she was? A lady? No one had ever called her that before.

"So, are we to be off to Inverness to search for your brothers now? Is that where you wish to go? I suppose you will be sorry to leave this place."

Annie looked around, at the stone walls and reached out to touch the one nearest her. It was cold and familiar as she knew it would be. She ran her fingers over it and pressed her palm against it.

"A little sorry, I suppose. But it has been my home for a while now. At least *it* hasn't changed even if everything around me has."

It began with a tickle and grew into a strange pulsating rhythm, like the beating of a heart. She couldn't bear to pull her hand away. From inside the wall came a buzzing. She remembered she had felt it once with Coblaith. She moved closer and put her ear to the stone.

The captain was watching her intently. He was waiting for her to speak.

The space around her was suddenly muffled in Annie's ears. The captain's voice was lost in a vacuum. A new voice came from inside the wall. No, it wasn't a *new* voice but an *old* one. Annie lips curled upward into a smile. She had learned the secret; she had finally inherited the gift from Coblaith. The stones were speaking to her, but it was the old druid's voice she heard, giving her wise counsel. Now she knew that wherever she went she would always have a connection, a muse, a spirit to follow.

"What is it?" It was the captain's voice finally breaking through the veil.

The wall went silent, and she turned toward him, leaning in close, yearning to have him take her in his arms.

"I think you and I should go on an adventure. Like the gypsies! We will sleep under the stars and bathe in the rivers and eat what the earth can provide."

The captain laughed out loud.

Annie leaned even closer and looked into his eyes. He could see the passion burning in hers. Without a word he put his arms around her and kissed her, deeply and slowly. When he pulled away, he could see she had tears streaming down her face.

"Those are tears of happiness I hope," he whispered.

Annie nestled her head against his shoulder.

"Aye," she said, "I am very happy."

EPILOGUE

When the horse had recovered, Annie and the captain continued their adventure travelling first to Inverness where Annie laid flowers on the battlefield in honor of her brother and the captain found temporary work on the docks. They then travelled south, to the lowlands of Aberdeenshire, where they married on March 5, 1747, in Pitsligo, started a farm, and raised a family. They remained in Pitsligo for the rest of their lives and are buried with their children in Peathill Kirkyard there. They were my ninth great grandparents.

As for Urquhart Castle, it was ultimately the Grant clan who retained control. Even though there were no attempts made to restore it, Caroline Stuart, the Dowager Countess of Seafield and wife of John Charles Grant had pity on the old castle and took pains to preserve it to keep it from falling further into disrepair. When she died, she instructed it be put under state care and to the present day its upkeep and maintenance has been in the hands of the Commissioner of the Queen. It has been one of Scotland's most visited tourist attractions.

When Annie died in 1788 and was laid to rest beneath the gothic structure that stood above the old kirkyard, there was a quiet funeral which only her children attended, the captain having died eleven years before. It was during that solemn service that something very strange and haunting occurred.

Sitting precariously atop the gable roof of the old church on Peathill was a square bell cot that had housed the bell that pealed whenever there was a death in the town of Pitsligo. It was called a *mort bell*, meaning *a sign of death*. But, after one too many storms over the centuries, the bell inside the structure had fallen and shattered into the graveyard below and had never been replaced for lack of funds.

On the day Annie was buried her children were surprised when, just as the grave keeper began pitching earth in the hole over her coffin, a bell began to ring ever so softly. No one at the ceremony knew where the sound was coming from. It was a mystery even to the clergymen of the church. A week later, when her gravestone was being put in place, the workman who was handling it felt a strange sensation coming through his fingers, moving up his arm. He could only explain it as something ghostly, and perhaps it was. Her children came forward and they could feel it too. There was a spirit there. Was it Annie's spirit or something else?

Coblaith would have told them that it was just the stones speaking.

The spirit in the stones.

Printed in Great Britain
by Amazon

13479086R00120